'I loooo   )k-   s   and funny, I
couldn   re.   \   ommend!!'

Amina, aged 12

'Hilarious, funny novel: impossible to put down!'

Olivia, aged 13

'*India Smythe in Love?* is not only relatable, hilarious and
heartwarming, but also raises important current issues!'

Mariel B, aged 17

'A very funny read – a thoroughly enjoyable book.
Highly recommended.'

Karan, aged 13

'Wonderful, witty, intriguing characters – India Smythe takes us
on another journey that many teenagers will relate to!'

Tabitha, aged 12

'This was such an enjoyable, easy to read book. I can really
relate to India's thoughts and feelings as a teenage girl.'

Izzy W, aged 14

'Relatable, realistic, and fun. I also think it is an accurate
description of how a lot of people reacted to coronavirus.
Because it has only been 6 or 7 months since it started, I
haven't come across any fiction that mentions it, but I think
that this felt similar to how my friends and I reacted.'

Ebba W, aged 13

'*India Smythe in Love?* talks about all types of relationships –
friendships, love relationships, mother and daughter bonds,
parents to boyfriends relationships, teacher to student
relationships, which I loved reading about.'

Hadiqa T, aged 14

'Not like other teen romances which are often pure fantasy! It's
more grounded and realistic.'

nan M, aged 13

'A relatable, honest and sometimes gritty look at teen life, but it is optimistic and always keeps you hanging on for the next small drama in her friend group or the next joke she will make about her and her silly but true life!'

Tula, aged 13

Praise for India Smythe Stands Up:

'The new YA comedy teens need... when a book like *India Smythe Stands Up* comes along you need to get it into as many hands as possible'

Lucas Maxwell, BookRiot

'One of the funniest protagonists since ... well ... ever! She fits in with Bridget Jones and Georgia Nicolson. The perfect antidote to the grim, grey times in which we find ourselves'

Teen Librarian

'A genuinely laugh-out-loud funny book with a fresh authentic voice'

Teach Secondary Magazine

'Laugh-out-loud story with a thoughtful subtext'

Books for Keeps

'A very funny book that still manages to deal with the more serious issues of friendship, social media and bullying'

School Librarian Magazine

'So funny I couldn't put it down'

South Wales Evening Post Book of the Week

for my lovely godchildren
Elodie and Theo

India Smythe
in Love?

Sarah Govett

Marotte
www.marottebooks.com

First published in 2020
by Marotte Books Ltd
51 York Avenue, London SW14 7LQ

www.marottebooks.com
Text © Sarah Govett 2020

The author asserts her moral right to be identified as author in accordance with
the Copyright, Designs and Patent Act, 1988

Typeset by Elaine Sharples
Printed and bound by PULSIO SARL

Cover illustration based on original artwork by Nina Duckworth

Overall cover design by Anne Glenn

There were only five more minutes left of school before the Christmas holidays.

The last lesson of the day was Chemistry, my current least-favourite subject. That's not fair. I actually like Chemistry, I just don't like our new Chemistry teacher, Mr Harold. He's got long, thin, orange hair tied up in a ponytail that drapes down the back of his jacket like a dead animal. He wears black shirts under a black suit and looks like he used to be in a really lame heavy metal band. Lisa asked him once, 'Were you in a band?' and he said, 'Oh...? No,' but with a smirk on his face as if looking like he'd been in a band made him really cool or something. Then Lisa said, 'So why do you dress like you're in a band then?' and that wiped the smile off his face.

The reason I don't like Mr Harold is that he's done some sort of advanced training in 'motivational learning' and the Chemistry lab is now covered in 'inspirational' posters. Where there used to be a periodic table there's now a diagram of a 'learning mountain'. When he first arrived at school after half term, Mr Harold told us to think of him as our 'mountain leader', shepherding us out of the 'trough of disillusionment' towards the 'slope of enlightenment'. And apparently the best way for that to happen was for us to get as much stuff wrong as possible, as:

'That way, you're learning!'

Anyway, as I said, it was five minutes to the bell and Mr Harold asked a really easy question to do with covalent bonds and my hand shot up of its own accord.

Stupid, stupid hand. Meena shot me a *what are you doing?* look.

Ever since Lisa's Christmas Party and the whole singing in the Christmas Concert evening I've been trying to keep a low profile and basically remain invisible. I've even been training myself to breathe more quietly. It's one thing achieving social enlightenment and realising that bullies like Lisa and April are not worth bothering about; it's another thing living that realisation at school. I'm sure even the Buddha might have fled into the toilets occasionally if he'd seen Lisa and April sashaying round the corner with an evil glint in their eyes.

Anyway, up my hand went and this is what happened next:

Mr Harold:	Yes, India?
Me:	A covalent bond involves sharing electrons.
Mr Harold:	(*Disappointed, not even a half smile*): Correct.

Lisa and April: Cough – LOSER – cough.

I kept my eyes on my desk to avoid their death stares. Mr Harold tried again.

'And does sodium chloride contain covalent bonds?'

Jasmine Wang put up her hand. Jasmine Wang is really good at Chemistry. Mr Harold ignored her and instead chose Jenny Weir to answer. Jenny Weir is rubbish at Chemistry.

Mr Harold: Yes, Jenny.
Jenny Weir: Um… (her voice is wavering, it's a 50:50 question, which way to go…) … Yes!
Mr Harold: (*Massive beaming smile*) It doesn't actually. But well done – you got it wrong – and that means you're learning!!

The bell rang and me and Meena headed out of the school gates to meet Anna and Gillian. Gillian's sort of become one of our gang now. Meena wasn't so keen at first – Gillian takes a bit of getting used to. Like liquorice. Or Marmite.

We were all going to go to Jump Zone. Anna's

suggestion, but me and Meena love it there too and Gillian, initially doubtful, was all up for it once she realised that it was a trampoline park, so basically sport, and that one of the trampolines even had a netball post at the end.

I asked them to give me ten minutes.

'Why?' from Anna.

'To see her *boy-friend* of course,' Meena replied, handing me a piece of gum at the same time. Good call. I'd had some of her Monster Munch for lunch.

Gillian rolled her eyes in disgust.

'He's not my boyfriend,' I said quietly.

'Of course he is!' Meena retorted. 'You've seen him every day after school since the concert.'

'But for, like, five minutes,' I countered. Which is true, but it's not through choice.

My parents grounded me when they saw me kissing Rich Evans backstage at the concert, so all I've been able to squeeze in is a tiny 'hi' and then 'bye' to get home with their being none the wiser. I'm not sure that counts. But then I started thinking about it. How do you know if you're actually going out with someone rather than just 'seeing them' a.k.a. randomly snogging them occasionally? Do you have to actually *say the words*: Do you want to be my boyfriend?

Anna:	Yes. Clarity is always good.
Meena:	No. Never say that.
Gillian:	I don't care.

Great. Really helpful, coherent advice. Thanks guys!

I walked up towards the gates to St Joseph's and waited for Rich to appear, praying to God that I wouldn't bump into Anthony and Ennis. The last time I'd seen Ennis was as I walked away from him at Lisa's party with a pretty cool, sarcastic 'Laterz', so I doubt he was going to be my number one fan.

The Year 7s came out first. Then the Year 8s and 9s. I kept waiting, pretending to be particularly interested in some car wheels and then a holly bush so I didn't look like a weirdo stalker. The chewing gum was starting to lose its flavour. I might as well have been chewing a piece of Blu-Tack. I searched my pockets but had nothing to spit it out into. Finally I saw him. Rich Evans. My Rich Evans. Big smile, deep dimples and that majestic forehead.

His smile was infectious and I couldn't help but smile back. I was so pleased to see him, I didn't even remember to turn to give him my good angle.

'Hi,' he said.

'Hi,' I said back. He tipped his chin towards me to kiss me and I raised my face to his. As our lips touched

5

I remembered too late that I still had the piece of gum in my mouth. I had never kissed a boy with gum in my mouth before. But people do, right? All the time. So I didn't panic too much.

Rich was kissing me, his tongue poking everywhere, and then, suddenly, I realised something.

There was no longer any gum in my mouth.

The gum had gone. *Where the hell had the gum gone?* I was pretty sure I hadn't swallowed it. I'm really careful not to swallow gum as, when I was about eight, my mum, who hates gum, told me that if you swallow it, it can block your oesophagus and then you can never eat again and will starve to death. Total rubbish. I looked it up. But I'm still a bit paranoid about it having been brainwashed so young. So the question remained – where was the gum?

At that moment Rich pulled away and looked at me rather strangely. He had a slightly disturbed look on his face. He was chewing something. Then it dawned on me. Oh God. He'd got my gum. He was now chewing my gum.

'Um … sexy,' he said, his voice rising at the end like a question. As in: *Is this supposed to be sexy?*? Aggghhhh. He'd thought I'd intentionally tongue-passed my flavourless Blu-Tack gum to him and he was meant to pretend to enjoy it.

'That wasn't meant to happen,' I said, staring at a crack in the pavement, willing it to widen and swallow me whole. 'Sorry.'

'That's OK,' he said stiffly, equally fascinated by the pavement.

There was an awkward pause. Our first awkward pause as a maybe-couple.

'Um ... is it OK if I take it out now?' Rich asked. 'The gum, I mean.'

'Um ... yes, sure.'

I was now the colour of a postbox. I could probably be seen from space by an alien using an infrared sensor.

Silent seconds stretched and dragged.

'Are you sure you don't want to hang out now?' Rich asked eventually.

'I can't,' I replied, meeting his eyes again. They were deep blue and crinkly and despite the horrors of the last few minutes they made me want nothing more than to spend these first few non-grounded hours with him. 'I promised Meena and the guys.'

I've always hated girls who bin their friends as soon as they meet a guy and I'd sworn to the gang that I wasn't going to be like that.

There was a pause again.

'OK, well, see you later, then.'

He didn't bend down to kiss me. Maybe he was

worried I had a second piece of flavourless stealth gum I'd try to slip his way.

I turned to walk back to my friends, wondering how I'd already managed to mess up something that had started so well, when I heard his voice calling me back.

'India … India?'

I swivelled and Rich was standing right behind me, eyes earnest, hair blown up by the wind, lengthening his forehead even further.

'Yes?'

'Do you want to be my girlfriend or something?' He was fidgeting from one foot to the other and looked like he'd rather be anywhere else in the world right now.

There was no awkward pause this time.

'Yes, yes I do.'

And then he relaxed and smiled again.

And I felt like the luckiest girl in the world.

Jump Zone was brilliant. Everyone found the gum swap incident annoyingly hilarious and I wished I hadn't told them but there's something about bouncing around on trampolines that makes you feel awesome and able to forgive anything and anyone. They should include compulsory trampoline breaks when they're negotiating international peace treaties.

The territory's mine!

No, it's mine!

And bounce.

Let's share it.

The other thing making me feel pretty great was obviously the fact that I now officially have a boyfriend.

Let me introduce you to Rich Evans – my boyfriend.

Are you together?

Yes, we are. He's my boyfriend.

Meena couldn't quite take it in at first.

'And this was before the whole gum swap thing?'

'No, after.'

'Are you sure?'

'One hundred percent.'

'Wow. He must really like you.'

So when I got home at 8pm – ('Let's see whether you can manage that, India, before we let you out any later') – Agghhh – I expected to have a bit of a relax in front of Netflix before heading to bed.

It didn't turn out quite like that.

I only got to watch fifteen minutes of TV and then had to head upstairs because Mum and Dad started the fight to end all fights. Caused by – you'd never guess it – an episode of *The Good Place*.

Mum enjoyed the show so much the first time round that she's making me and Dad watch it all from the beginning. She says it's because 'the philosophical dilemmas it raises are fascinating'. Really it's because she's got a crush on the guy who plays Chidi.

Anyway, we were watching the one where they talk about the trolley problem – basically if a train was hurtling down a track towards a few people, would you pull a lever to send it off in another direction to kill just one person instead? Nothing that argument-inducing you might think. Wrong. Enter slightly insecure Mum.

Mum: Would you pull a lever to divert a train away from me?

Dad: (*Smiling, thinking he's on safe ground*) Of course, my love.

Mum: What about if it meant sending it towards more people?

Dad: (*Still smiling, the fool*) I'd still do it. I couldn't lose you, babe.

Mum: What if it meant sending it towards a really large group of people?

Dad: (*The smile starting to fade*) Yeesss.

Mum: What about if it meant sending it towards the whole of France?

Mum's got a thing about France at the moment. Her new boss, who's French, is giving her a hard time.

Dad: (*Smile completely gone*) Errrr…

And that was his crime.
To hesitate before agreeing to the genocide of the entire population of France.

Mum: Sometimes I can't believe you, Andy.
Dad: It's just there are an awful lot of people in France…
Mum: Well, it's good to know how you feel.
Dad: About sixty-seven million. I just looked it up on my phone. See … here … sixty-seven million.
Mum: I don't want to talk to you right now. I don't want to even look at you.

And then it went on from there.
Unbelievable.
I don't think however serious me and Rich get that I'll ever ask him to murder an entire country to save me.
Well, definitely not a country as big as France anyway.
Liechtenstein maybe.
But not France.

I'm seeing Rich tomorrow afternoon – my parents finally gave in and agreed I could meet up with him on condition that (a) it was in public and (b) I was home by seven ('So that pervert doesn't try anything!' – *thanks, Dad*). This is going to be the only time I get to see him before Christmas as his mum's then whisking him away to a remote bit of Wales to see his cousins. The reason this is relevant is: tomorrow I have to give him a present.

I had no clue what to buy and I didn't want to choose all by myself so I called in the gang and we met for lunch in Rainston. Difficult decisions call for highly calorific food so we got a table at Burger Burger Burger and ordered cheeseburgers and fries all round. When Anna finally finished a particularly long story about something not very interesting that happened in orchestra, it was my chance to pick their brains.

Me: So, what do you think I should get Rich for Christmas?

Meena: (Authoritatively) Something sexy.

I felt as confused as Anna looked. Gillian rolled her eyes in disgust.

Me: What do you mean … sexy?

Meena: You know … sexy.

Me: No, I don't know.

There was no use pretending – I was completely out of my depth.

Meena: (*Shrugging casually*) Underwear or something.

Me: Isn't that what boys get girls?

Meena: That's so sexist.

Me: So I should get Rich underwear?

Meena: Yeah. Sexy tight boxers or something.

I tried to imagine me handing Rich a box with some tight black boxers in while batting my eyelids suggestively. I felt sick inside. I was perfectly happy snogging him. I didn't want to give him boxers. I didn't even really want to see him in his boxers. The thought was starting to give me palpitations. I needed help. Meena hadn't delivered so I turned to … Anna.

Anna: Something engraved. You know, with his initials on. Guys like it when things have their initials on.

Do they? *Do they really?* Anna seemed super sure about this. She may not have ever had a boyfriend, but she does have a brother. Meena has a brother too and she wasn't dissing the idea.

Gillian: And trophies. Everyone likes trophies.

I looked at Meena. She was staring at her fries.

Me: ...So I should get a trophy?
Anna: With his initials on.

The tiny seed of hope I had that we were getting somewhere shrivelled up and died. If I followed their advice I'd basically be buying a trophy engraved R.E.

And the prize for best work in Religious Education goes to...

I love my friends but sometimes they are no use whatsoever.

In the end I bought him a cap. Not a rubbish cap or anything. It was made of grey wool and would suit his eyes. Plus it would push his curls down so his forehead didn't have to look quite so majestic all of the time.

I couldn't help but feel pretty pleased with myself. I'd done it. I'd bought him a present I think he'll like. I'd put a bit of thought into it. I didn't follow the terrible advice of my friends and buy him a trophy. All in all – good job, India.

I wonder what he's bought me?

Present swap day.

I'd arranged to meet Rich in a café in the village. I got there five minutes early and was about to do an unnecessary lap of the Green to kill time and calm my nerves about handing over the present (the cap had seemed like less and less of a good idea the closer to the café I'd got) when I spotted him already inside. Damn. I had no choice but to enter. As I walked towards him I spotted a rectangular present in green wrapping paper sat on the table in front of him and a smile popped onto my face. It was the size and shape of a book. He clearly hadn't gone the sexy underwear route either. Or the romantic jewellery option. A book. A cap could compete with a book. We were on an equal footing.

I sat opposite him and looked at the menu. He was having a milkshake. I was tempted but managed to resist. The last thing I needed was another sugar-crazed Patrick Swayze hallucination.

'Just a tea, please.'

We chatted for a while. He told me about his cousins and how much he was looking forward to seeing them.

'We always get together and just jam in Fred's garage.'

'Oh, I thought you just played the cello?'

'I do. We jam on the cello, oboe and flute.'

Right…

'But I'm going to miss you so much,' he said earnestly, leaning forward and kissing me, and I forgot all about his geekiness. When a guy was this nice, he could 'jam' wearing stick-on elf-ears and everything would still be OK. Maybe OK. If the pointy bits were very subtle.

'And I got you this.'

He thrust the present across the table towards me.

'Open it.'

I didn't quite get why he was so keen on me unwrapping a book in front of him, but I obliged anyway, ripping open the green paper. And then I saw it. A hardback copy of *The Jungle Book*. A beautiful version. I leafed through it. The illustrations were works of *Art*.

'Because of the concert,' he said. I nodded. I'd got it – the Christmas Concert where we'd got together because I'd joined him on stage singing *I Wan'na Be Like You*.

It was the most perfect, thoughtful, romantic present anyone had ever bought me.

And I'd got him a cap.

'Thanks. Thanks so much,' I stammered. He was beaming with pleasure, dimples deepening. They could fit a cherry, snugly.

'I wrote in it too,' he offered, shyly, turning to the dedication page.

For India,

The best do-be-doer I've ever met.

Love Rich.

I was staring at the words *'Love Rich'*. Was he just signing off like 'Love Granny' or did it mean something more? Was he saying he was in love with me already? It was too soon, wasn't it? I didn't want him to go all psycho stalker on me, not that he seemed the type. To tell the truth I was flattered. Deeply flattered that I could have that effect on someone so quickly.

Then Rich registered me staring at the words *'Love Rich'* and everything went weird and still and static.

'Oh God … I didn't mean it like that!' he burst out. 'I don't *love* you. That'd be weird. That'd be far too soon… I mean I *like* you. I *really* like you. But I'm not saying I *love* you … *now*. God. Sorry to freak you out. Does that make you feel better?'

Better knowing that my boyfriend definitely doesn't love me? Hmmm…

The waitress came over.

'Can I get you anything else?'

'Um … no thanks.'

She left again and I stared deep into my mug as if trying to read the tea leaves. They probably would have had a lot to stay if they weren't stuck inside a PG Tips tea bag. Looking up again I saw that Rich was staring expectantly at the wrapped gift by my side. The cap. The really not very thoughtful, totally unromantic cap.

I took a deep breath. 'I got this for you,' I said, passing it over. 'You don't have to open it now.'

'Oh no, I want to. Part of the fun of giving people things is seeing their reaction, don't you think?'

No, not when it's a cap, I don't.

Rich unwrapped the present slowly, as if he was teasing it open. When he pulled out the cap he looked confused, turning it over and looking inside and at the label to see what exactly the cap signified. What was the secret message, the thoughtful gesture to be discovered? When he finally realised that there wasn't one, that sometimes a cap is just a cap, he forced a smile and put it on his head.

'Thanks, India. I love it.'

We split the bill and then he walked me back to my bus stop. It was outside a cobbler's. He put his arm round me while we waited and we both stared in through the cobbler's window as something to do. In pride of place was a sign advertising 'engravings while you wait'. Under the sign sat a small silver trophy.

'Cool trophy,' Rich said wistfully.

For God's sake.

Lunch at Aunty Hope's.

We do this every 23rd December. No one enjoys it. It's pure obligation. But at least it means there's Christmas Eve to get back into that holiday mood before the big day.

'Why don't we do it at ours this year?' Mum had suggested to her sister on the phone a month back.

'Oh, how sweet. But our house is *so much bigger*, it just makes more sense.'

Cue broken plate in the bin next time I looked.

Aunty Hope only lives about twenty minutes' drive away, but the journey seemed to last forever as Mum and Dad were bickering so much in the front.

'Remember, your practice is doing really well,' instructed Mum.

'It *is* doing well,' Dad replied, confused.

'But *really* well… And I'm set for a promotion at work,' Mum continued.

'Oh that's brilliant news, Sammy!' Dad burbled.

Mum rolled her eyes at the moron that she'd married.

'It's all in the wording. "Set for" sounds good but legally means nothing.'

So Aunty Hope is less likely to sue you???

'Just follow my lead. This lunch isn't going to rise anyone's soufflé. We just have to get through it. In. Out. Don't curdle the eggs.'

Me and Dad stared at her.

'What? *What?*' she said, all defensive. 'It's a saying.'

No it's not. But we both bit our lips and nodded. Now was not the time to mock her ridiculous self-created baking-based phrases.

There was nowhere to park outside their house so we had to park at the end of the road. As we got out the car, Mum glared at the road sign: Elm Avenue. It's another of her petty grievances that Aunty Hope lives on an 'Avenue' rather than a common 'Street' like us.

'Some day, I'd like to live on an Avenue, too, Andrew,' she said last year as she stomped away from their house.

'There's no difference,' Dad had replied, confused. 'They're both just road names.'

'Oh, Andrew. You don't understand anything.'

We traipsed towards their house, stopping for a deep breath at the bottom of their drive. There was a beat as we all stared up at the house.

Annoyingly, their house *is* much bigger than ours. And classier. Even their outside lights are 'warm white' and twinkle like real stars whereas ours (chosen and put up by Dad last week) are blue and flash. There should be a warning sign for passers-by. *This house may trigger epilepsy.*

Mum's knuckles were white as she clutched the extra-large box of Ferrero Rocher in her left hand.

'United front,' she hissed before ringing the bell. 'We are a successful and happy family.'

Were we not? God, what did Mum really think about us?

The door opened and there was Aunty Hope. A prettier, younger-looking, better-hair-cut version of Mum (although she's actually two years older). It was like a permanent dagger in Mum's side. Just behind her stood my cousin, Willow. A prettier, older-looking version of me (although she's actually one year younger). Thinner. With three hundred and sixty degrees of good angle, bigger boobs and a smug face. I felt annoyance bubble up inside and a weird empathy towards Mum.

'Nigel, the SmITHs are here,' Aunty Hope called upstairs. It was Dad's turn to tense up. Ever since he confessed to them two Christmases ago (after a third glass of wine) that his parents had changed the family name from Smith to Smythe, Aunty Hope takes particular glee in calling us the SmITHs.

'And how are you, Andy? she asked, ushering us inside. 'Or is it Andrew now? I find it so hard to keep up.'

'I'm very well, thank you,' Dad replied between gritted teeth. 'Really, really successful and happy.'

Mum thrust the box of Ferrero Rocher into Aunty Hope's hands, who looked at it, faintly surprised before putting it on the windowsill.

'Oh … how kind. And clever finding these. I had no idea they still made them.'

Aunty Hope then disappeared into the kitchen to fetch her smoked salmon blinis 'fresh, not store bought, *of course*' and me and Willow stared at different corners of the living room. If we didn't make eye contact, we didn't have to talk.

Lunch was horrific. Not the food. The food was really good. Beef stew and then individual crème caramels. Aunty Hope is a much better cook than Mum, something else Mum finds really hard to deal with. Every time Mum took a mouthful her face was wracked with competing emotions: yum, this is delicious versus aggggghhhh damn her this is delicious.

But it was difficult to focus on the food. It was a mere backdrop. To war. A war that had been feuding for at least as many years as I've been alive, and a war that the Smythes/Smiths showed no chance of being able to win.

Aunty Hope drew blood first, bringing up Uncle Nigel's recent pay rise.

'...Not enough to buy a chalet, of course, but let's just say we could rent one for a long time. Or maybe buy one ... if it was a bit on the small side.'

Mum parried with an inspiringly vague spiel about her imaginary promotion.

Dad tried to help too, but he shouldn't have done. He was out of his depth.

'We could probably rent a chalet too,' he offered. 'Although not at February half-term. I've heard prices are ridiculous then. Christmas too. We'd probably have to take India out of school in the middle of term.'

Mum stared daggers at Dad who then followed Uncle Nigel's example and sat chewing his exceptionally tender beef in silence.

Their own achievements exhausted, talk turned to me and Willow.

Aunty Hope kept on going on about how AMAZINGLY well Willow was doing at school. 'Oxbridge material, the teachers say.' So Mum started talking me up too. It was excruciating.

'"Gifted" is the word they use most about India...' (*They don't.*) 'Set for straight 9s at GCSE.' (*I'm not.*)

'Willow is a natural athlete. She's county-level in three sports.'

'India performed a solo at the Christmas recital.'(*As a volunteer to appease a boy I liked.*)

'Willow is the lead in the school play.'

'India…' Mum faltered. She'd run out of made-up stuff too early. Frankly, I was a bit offended. Parents are supposed to dote on their children. Especially when they're only children. So why couldn't she think of any other good thing to say about me, real or imaginary?

Mum was starting to shake with mental effort. *What to say, what to say…* She looked in desperation at my dad. You didn't need to be a mind reader to understand her internal scream: *Help me*!

'India,' Dad suddenly exploded, '…has a wonderful new boyfriend.'

I was so shocked I swallowed a far too big spoonful of crème caramel whole and then was coughing with tears coming out of my eyes.

We left soon after.

No one talked for the first ten minutes of the drive home. It was only when we were on the A3 that Mum broke the silence.

'Well, India,' she said, pretending to be upbeat. 'After Christmas I suppose we'd better properly meet this *wonderful* new boyfriend of yours, then.'

And I'd thought the day couldn't get any worse.

Christmas day itself is a bit underwhelming once you've grown out of the whole Santa thing. There are still presents, obviously. And nice food. But the *can't sleep from excitement/bounce out of bed really early* aspect totally goes, so Mum bringing in a cup of tea at 8am wasn't met with the appreciation she seemed to think it deserved.

Mum: (*Almost ripping the curtains off the rail in enthusiasm*) Happy Christmas, India!
Me: Erhhh. Mmmmmm.
Mum: Come on India, make an effort!

And I thought Christmas was meant to be all about the kids.

Mum left and, groaning, I pulled myself out of bed, picked up the half-full pillowcase from the end of my bed and trudged down the corridor. My parents still like me to open my stocking in their room.

'What's Santa brought you? *Wink wink,*' Dad chuckled as if he hadn't said the same thing for the last five years in a row. It isn't even 100% a joke. Mum buys all the presents for me so he doesn't actually have a clue what's inside.

Stifling a massive yawn, I reached into the stocking and started unwrapping.

Some chocolate – *good*.

An orange – *expected*.

A pack of five neon highlighters – *fair enough*.

Headphones – *surprisingly good*.

A three-pack of nude knickers – size large – *terrible, terrible, terrible*.

For so many reasons.

Firstly, they weren't my skin colour. I have very pale skin. These were beige. Meaning they weren't 'nude', giving the illusion of sexy bare skin at all – they looked like I had actively chosen to wear beige pants. The least sexy colour of all time. Secondly, I do not wear 'large' knickers. There is nothing wrong with wearing large or extra-large knickers if that's your size. But, if like me, you are medium size, large knickers result in a weird, baggy silhouette. If there's anything less sexy than beige underwear, it's baggy, beige underwear.

'They look nice and comfy,' Mum offered.

Dad had gone a strange non-beige colour and suddenly had to leave the room.

Next was breakfast. To the sound of Michael Bublé. It's been pretty non-stop Bublé for the last ten days. I'm pretty much Bublé-d out. Breakfast was coffee and panettone – which is like an Italian cake bread with raisins in. It's really nice. We've never had it at home before – we usually have toast with Nutella as a special treat for Christmas – but I remember Aunty Hope making a point of saying they always have it. It's 'the sophisticated Christmas breakfast'.

'This is nice,' I mumbled between mouthfuls.

'Yes, it's what we always have for Christmas.'

No it's not. How did she think she could get away with saying that? I live here too.

Even Dad choked on some crumbs.

Mum popped a capsule into her Nespresso machine while Dad spooned some Nescafé into a mug.

'Which will it be, India?' he said. 'Mum's rubbish or the good stuff?'

Ever since I went out for my bonding coffee with Mum a few weeks back, they've allowed me to have a mug every now and then, realising that it might not destroy my 'sensitive developing nervous system' after all.

'Nespresso,' I replied immediately and Dad rolled his eyes.

'You people. You don't know what you're missing.'

After breakfast we got to open our main presents. Mum likes us to open them one at a time so we can 'share the excitement'.

Mum had got Dad some binoculars to go with his

new tragic interest in bird watching. He seemed genuinely thrilled.

'Look at the magnification on these babies,' he whistled in appreciation. 'And so lightweight and portable.' *Oh, Dad, your younger self would be so ashamed right now.*

Dad gave Mum her present from him. It was beautifully wrapped – clearly by some in-store-wrapping person, not him.

She pulled off the layers daintily and then gave a squeal of delight. Inside, on a bed of silver tissue paper sat some butt-sculpting leggings decorated with strawberry ice-cream colour leopard print and lace detailing around the knee. Hideous.

'I love them!' she was laughing. 'Oh, it's so funny.' *Why?* 'Nothing, you'll see. Oh what a hoot!' *No one else is laughing.* 'These will look great with my pink angora cardie.' Great. The cardie that stops at her waist, again, so another, full on butt-baring outfit for my mum. *Good work, Dad.*

'Oh, I can't wait any longer!' Mum giggled, thrusting me my present from them. Far less beautifully wrapped. I looked down at it, wondering why Mum was acting so weirdly. Warily I pulled apart the paper to be confronted with … black Lycra … strawberry leopard print … lace knee detail … NO! Matching hers-and-hers active wear.

Was I trapped in some level of hell? A particularly fiery one. Mum started laughing again.

'You said you wanted to do more sport!'

I don't remember that.

'We can go out for another girls' coffee together in them!'

NO.

'Or a speed walk in the park!'

NO.

'Maybe people will think we're sisters?!'

Aggghhhhhhhhh.

This Christmas truly sucks.

'Half an hour till we leave!' Dad yelled up the stairs.

We were having Christmas lunch at Nan and Grandad's.

I don't take very long to get ready so I threw on some jeans and a top, tied my hair up and then started texting the gang. I got a really sweet text from Rich:

'Miss you, sexy. I wanna be with you-oo-oo. Happy Christmas! xxx'

I was in the middle of texting something back when Mum shouted at me to get in the car.

'Is that what you're wearing? For Christmas lunch?' she said as I came down the stairs. She clearly disapproved of my outfit. 'You don't take a Victoria sponge to a cake show.'

'We don't all have gold sequin tops, Mum,' I replied, perhaps a bit too sarcastically. I shouldn't have worried. Water off a duck's back.

'I suppose not. Well, maybe I could get you one for your birthday?'

Dear God.

Dad was wearing some sort of smart trousers with a crease ironed down the front and an ironed, tucked-in shirt and tie. He looked like he was going for a job interview. He always likes to dress up when we visit his parents. Show them how well he's done.

It took about forty-five minutes to get there and it was another unrelaxing car ride. Mum always gets stressed when we're going to Nan and Grandad's. 'No one's good enough for their little boy.' When she gets stressed, her back straightens and she seems to grow a few centimetres. You don't realise till you see it, but she must normally have terrible posture. A real huncher.

I tried to text Rich from the car, but Mum exploded with something about it being 'family time' so instead we just sat in awkward family silence for the next twenty minutes.

Nan and Grandad's house was visible from the end of the road. And probably from space. There was a light-up Santa and sleigh parked in their front garden, surrounded by flashing blue lights so intense that the whole area seemed to pulsate. Seems like tacky light choice is genetic, fading slightly from generation to generation. Maybe I'm destined to still buy blue ones but they'll just glow.

'Your mother really has terrible taste,' Mum muttered.

'Try to be nice,' Dad muttered back.

While we were walking up the path to the front door I realised that this was my chance to finally finish that text to Rich. He'd be thinking I was ignoring him. I quickly pulled out my phone. Odd. Appeared I'd sent one.

Or rather my pocket using the power of predictive text combined with random button pressing had.

'Happy birthday cvvv%%%erty to rrrrrrrrrrh12'

No. No. No.

My phone beeped.

Rich again.

'Don't quite get it? x'

'Put your phone away, India! This is why we can't give you a smart phone. You're already addicted.'

She didn't stop there though. She swiped my phone

out of my hand and put it in her bag. Leaving me with no way of showing my boyfriend I wasn't a complete loser weirdo.

Before I had a chance to respond, Grandad opened the door with a massive smile on his face.

'The Sm-I-I-I-I-I-I-thes are here!' he yelled into the kitchen.

'I'm turning the turkey! Show them round!' Nan yelled back.

Every time we go to Nan and Grandad's we have to 'have the tour' – see any minor bit of remodelling they've done or 'interior design touches' they've added – 'The blue silk flowers really lift the room, don't you think?' – plus admire Dad's old room that is still decked out like a psycho shrine to his younger self.

Dad winning a minor running race.

Dad (with terrible acne) in his first band.

Dad getting a 'positive participant' rosette in a chess tournament.

'He could have had any girl, your dad,' Grandad sighed wistfully.

Mum's back straightened even further. She might be a natural five foot nine.

We returned to the lounge and Nan finally emerged from the kitchen.

And suddenly the whole day took a turn for the better.

It was like everything suddenly went slow motion.

Nan appearing.

Mum's mouth dropping open.

Nan's eyes lighting up.

Mum's face crumpling.

Nan's face beaming.

Yes ... they were wearing matching gold sequin tops.

We left as soon as lunch was over.

'You don't know how I feel,' Mum spluttered as we turned out the drive.

Oh yes, Mum, I do. I really do.

I called Rich from my room when I got in and explained about my weirdo text and everything. He wasn't mad – he just found it funny. He's such a great guy. But he couldn't talk for long. Jam session was starting in five and he had to tune his cello.

Feeling strangely hungry despite having done very little apart from eat all day, I went downstairs at six for food and Mum seemed really down. Dad was stroking her hair as she was half-sobbing, 'I don't know why I bother... India makes no effort ... your mother ...'

I was going from victim to oppressor and the

annoying thing was that Mum's guilt trip was working. I know Christmas is really special to her – her parents died around Christmas when she was youngish – and I hadn't been making the greatest of efforts. I needed to cheer her up...Unfortunately there was only one way I knew how.

I tiptoed upstairs again and stared at the offending garment, still lying in its torn-open wrapping paper. Maybe they looked better on? Maybe not. Might as well go the whole hog. I opened the packet of large, beige knickers and, undressing first, obvs, put a pair on. No wriggling required. They looked horrific but, on the upside, they were surprisingly comfortable. Next came the leggings. I pulled them up, suppressing shudders of revulsion as I did so. The bum-sculpting technology hoisted the beige baggy pants up and squashed the excess pant material into weird, round folds so it looked like I had butt-based varicose veins or was smuggling garden worms. Short jumper on top as a final peace offering, I stared in the mirror.

Dear God.

Why oh why would anyone choose to wear this stuff? The worst, the very worst part was the knee lace detail. Don't try to make knees sexy. Knees are, like, the least sexy part of the body. Knees and elbows. They're bony. They stick out. They are functional joints. It's like putting make-up on a knuckle.

A couple more deep breaths for luck and a few *'you're doing this for Mum*'s later I padded downstairs to the kitchen.

'Fancy watching a movie, Mum?' I asked.

Mum took a second to look up, but when she did, her whole face lit up and everything was worth it.

'Oh, yes. Let's watch *Pretty Woman*. I'll just get my active wear on too.'

She was up the stairs in a flash and Dad smiled a 'thanks' in my direction.

We got through half a tub of Quality Streets as we watched the film. Even Dad was on his best behaviour. He merely flinched rather than blocked the screen when Julia Roberts produced her array of different-coloured condoms.

It was nice.

Actually, really nice.

The way Christmas is meant to be.

On my way up to bed, Mum called after me.

'India ... thanks for that.'

'That's OK. Sorry about before.'

There was a pause. I knew Mum wanted to say something else but was hanging back. She was staring weirdly at my behind.

'What is it, Mum?' I prompted.

'...It's just that maybe you should think about

35

wearing a longer top with your leggings. It's not the most … flattering silhouette on you.'

28th December. One of the most boring days in the whole calendar. I couldn't get hold of any of my friends, we'd run out of family to visit and my Christmas chocolate was nearly gone. Just some strawberry creams left. The chocolate equivalent of a clammy, limp handshake. But I still ate them. At 9:15am. They tasted even worse than usual, probably because of the accompanying soundtrack coming from the kitchen. Sounds can apparently affect taste. I read somewhere once that a top chef serves oysters with an iPod with sounds of the sea on. Ridiculous, I thought at the time. Now I'm not so sure. All I know is that strawberry creams definitely taste worst when consumed to the sound of Mum stirring cake batter and singing, 'My mad-el-eines bring all the boys to the yard.'

This afternoon I was so bored that I even asked Mum and Dad if they wanted to do something with me. They didn't. They were 'too busy', which I frankly found insulting. Mum, having completed every mindful colouring book on the market, has moved onto embroidery and was cross-stitching a really naff picture of a milkmaid on a bridge. Dad too 'couldn't be disturbed'. He was 'in his office' a.k.a. finishing the Lego Big Ben that he'd treated himself to as an extra Christmas present. '4163 pieces of fun,' he said longingly as he cradled the box.

'Why don't you revise?' Mum suggested as I huffed around the kitchen. In Year 10 we have tests at the start of every term. The idea is if we do exams all the time, we'll get better at them, and results are basically all that St Mary's cares about. But, even though I do actually care about getting good grades next year, I think it's necessary to get things in perspective. GCSEs are obviously important but everything leading up to that – less so. I doubt Mo Farah was going to be entering some Surrey Athletics Society long distance run and giving it his all. He'd be saving his energy for a race that actually mattered.

That said, I had nothing else to do so I made a revision timetable for the next few days. Revision is the worst but I do like making revision timetables. I used every single one of my new neon highlighters and the end result looked pretty awesome. I stuck it on my cork board and felt rather smug. It was pretty much like I'd done the revision already.

Next, I thought I'd try and actually learn some

Physics. Mr Harold did a whole Year 10 and 11 Assembly about revision techniques and one thing he was all over was mnemonic devices. Basically ways of making it easier to remember stuff. The obvious example he gave was colours of the rainbow: Richard Of York Gave Battle In Vain. Red Orange Yellow Green Blue Indigo Violet. Easy to remember. All good. This term we've been doing the electromagnetic spectrum so I thought it'd be good to come up with something equivalent for that.

I stared at the page.

Radio waves

Microwaves

Infrared

Visible light

Ultraviolet

X-rays

Gamma rays

So something R M I V U X G.

Not very inspiring. It was like looking at a set of Scrabble letters and knowing I was going to score about five points with 'rim'. Actually, I sell myself short. I could probably score six with 'mug'.

Focus. Hmmm…

Let's have a go.

Rachel's Mum…

And I ground to a halt.

Rachel's Mum…

Damn. That was now stuck in my head as the only possible start.

Rachel's Mum Is Very Ugly… I don't know where that came from, but I'm on a roll. A total roll! I might be coming up with a deeply unpleasant phrase that I can't share, but damn, it's good. Bonus is I only know one Rachel – Rachel Turner in 10E – and her mum's really pretty so no one will take it at face value. She turns up to parents' evenings in well-cut suit dresses and all the dads pretend not to stare.

Just X and G to go.

Hmmm…

Rachel's Mum Is Very Ugly … X (like kiss) Gillian.

OK, the last bit doesn't really make any sense, but I still did it. Electromagnetic spectrum consider yourself conquered. I am a mnemonics master. Time for a break.

As if on cue, my phone beeped. It was Gillian. She was going for a bike ride with Anna and did I want to join them? Yes, yes I did.

I stuffed on my trainers, grabbed my coat and a packet of Monster Munch, zipped the Monster Munch into my pocket, creating a weirdly bulky, lopsided silhouette, gave a quick explanation to Mum (who wasn't really listening as she was unpicking the milkmaid's bonnet that she'd done in mid-brown rather than the correct dark tan) and was out the door.

It was a fifteen-minute bike ride to where I was meeting Gillian and Anna so I was already a bit tired by the time I got there. Not that it mattered. 'Cycling' was code for meet up, go and sit somewhere outside and have a chat while sharing a packet of Monster Munch or two that the others had brought. Not normally having Monster Munch in the house myself, I usually had to bring some lame wholegrain baked snack that got eaten last, but this time was different. This time I had access to the good stuff. I chose Roast Beef flavour for a change, thinking Anna would most likely bring Pickled Onion and that way we could mix it up a bit.

I spotted Anna first. High-waisted jeans, red fleece pulled up to her neck and a bulging right pocket. Excellent. It took me a second to register Gillian. She was in head-to-toe dark green Lycra – serious Lycra (no lace knee detail) – and was, as such, almost camouflaged against the trees. Her helmet was securely fastened under her chin and her foot hadn't even left the pedal. It was resting there, ready to push off at a second's notice. Anna shot a worried look in my direction. She'd realised it too.

Gillian didn't speak code.

For Gillian, cycling meant cycling.

'You're wearing jeans too?' Gillian barked in annoyance as I stopped in front of them.

'Yes?'

'What about chafing?'

'Err…'

I didn't really understand what she meant. I've cycled in jeans before. Correction – I always cycle in jeans. I basically only ever wear jeans.

'I've planned a quick little 10K route,' Gillian explained.

Me and Anna both flinched. I didn't really know what 10K looked like, but it sounded far. Really far. I looked at Gillian to see if she was joking.

She wasn't. She was frowning, her monobrow becoming a thick straight line. Almost as if it was underlining quite how serious she was.

And then her right foot pressed down and she was off, without so much as a 'follow me'.

Me and Anna struggled after her, up hills, down hills, even off-road down some horrifically bumpy dirt track that wove in and out of trees. My heart was pumping crazy fast. Worryingly fast. If there'd been time to stop, I'd have asked Anna to get out her phone and google, 'Can too much exercise kill you?'

'Isn't this fun!' Gillian cried as she disappeared over the horizon.

'Do you think we can take a break?' Anna gasped next to me.

'I've no idea where we are,' I panted back. 'I don't want to end up lost in the woods, eaten by wild animals.'

'Not sure they're any wild animals here,' said Anna doubtfully.

'They're foxes, definitely,' I said.

'Yeah – foxes can be vicious,' she agreed.

So we kept going.

I'd never cycled so far before. Anna had never cycled so far before.

My legs hurt. My hands had blisters from gripping the brakes. And chafing. Yes, I now completely understood what chafing was. My inner thighs felt like they were on fire and it was no joke. I never wanted to wear jeans again.

Eventually, after what seemed like hours, we were back where we started.

'Same time tomorrow?' Gillian asked, grinning. She wasn't even out of breath. She was the most in-breath a person could be.

'Sorry, I'm busy,' Anna gasped.

'Me too,' I panted.

Gillian, her foot still perched on the pedal for readiness, took that as her sign to speed off and me and Anna just collapsed on the grass by the edge of the road.

We took out our packets of Monster Munch (shaken into crumbs by the ride) and shared out the salty goodness. Anna *had* brought Pickled Onion. A more comforting flavour, it turns out.

'Let's never go on a bike ride with Gillian again,' Anna said as we licked the packets clean.'

'Deal,' I replied.

When I got home I peeled my jeans off. I needed something soft to wear to rest my poor thighs. Something without seams.

Flinching inside, I pulled on the strawberry leopard print leggings once more and then went to curl up on the sofa downstairs.

Mum smiled as she walked past in matching gear.

'I knew you'd like them,' she beamed.

Is this how it all begins? Have I accidentally started on the slippery slope that leads to twenty-four-hour active wear?

God, I hope not.

But they are comfortable, I have to give her that. Far too comfortable.

Spent most of the day at Meena's. We were supposed to

be meeting in Rainston, but it was cold and wet and generally grim so Meena suggested hers instead.

It was such a relief to be out of the house. Dad was practising guitar in the garage and there's only so much mournful chords and voice cracking that a girl can take.

'Thought you were both busy today,' Gillian grunted as me and Anna turned up.

'Errr…' we both stammered.

'Don't worry, I'm only messing with you,' she said. 'I know you both hate cycling.'

Not cycling. I said in my head. *Cycling with you.*

The supposed point of meeting up was to plan New Year's Eve, but that was just an excuse. Some people get really stressy about New Year's Eve. Where they're going. Who they're going there with. Whether they'll have some guy to kiss at midnight.

We already knew what we were going to do. What we always did – go round to Anna's, eat pizza and watch movies.

Just girls. Food, films, friends. No one to impress. No one to try and snog (Rich was still in Wales).

The only things left to decide were which pizza toppings we wanted and what films we wanted to see.

Meena's mum had insisted on cooking for us so we ate first. She's an amazing cook and we hoovered up Roti, Daal, Sabzi, Samosas and then mango ice cream to finish. I ate so much I felt bloated and was pleased that Meena's brother Guv was out as he's quite hot and I didn't want him to see my little pot belly.

After lunch we all went up to Meena's room. She had a glint in her eye as she sat on her bed and I knew she had plans for us. Bitter experience has taught me to distrust that glint.

'Right, makeover time!' she declared.

I squealed like an animal in pain.

'No way!'

Last time Meena tried to give me a makeover, I'd ended up in horror-show make-up, hiding in a garden in the dark. I wasn't a total idiot. I learnt from my mistakes. Nothing Meena could say would make me let her do anything to me ever again.

'Suit yourself. I just thought you might be a bit self-conscious about those dark hairs on your upper lip.'

You've got to give it to her. Meena knows what buttons to push. Meena is a persuasive genius.

'What hairs?' I stammered. 'I don't have any hairs.' I'm not a Victorian in mourning who has draped every mirror in the house in a sheet. I know what I look like. I look at myself in the mirror every day. Morning and evening when I brush my teeth. Cautionary glance in the hall mirror before I leave the house. Mirrors in the toilets at school. Surely I'd have noticed something? Surely?

But then Meena delivered the killer blow. She whisked out this circular concave make-up mirror and thrust it in my face. I stared into its depths.

Mirror mirror on the wall…

Dear. God.

It was like looking at my face under a microscope. Every pore became a crater. My mole became a brown, craggy mountain. And the top of my lip became … hairy. Noticeable, dark-brown hairs. No No NO!

You are the hairiest of them all…

'Ignore her,' Gillian said, 'I can't see anything. No one looks at you that close up.'

She was right. *Listen to Gillian,* I told myself. *Gillian knows what's what.*

'Unless they're kissing you,' Meena added.

Damn, she'd done it again. She'd convinced me. Someone kissing you would see you really, really close up. Particularly around your mouth. And, now I had a bona fide boyfriend, I planned to do a lot of kissing.

'What do I do about it?' I squeaked. 'Make them go away, Meena. Make them go away.'

'That's what I'm here for,' she smiled, producing a facial bleaching kit, as if from thin air. 'I've used it before,' she said reassuringly. 'You just add the accelerator to the bleach, mix, apply, leave for ten minutes and then rinse off.'

It did sound really easy.

'And it definitely works?' I asked.

'Yes,' she replied with a firm nod of the head, exuding confidence. 'Every time.'

She added three scoops of bleach to one scoop of accelerator cream on this white plastic rectangle and then mixed it all together with something that looked like a glue spreader from primary school.

'Sit still,' she instructed and then painted a white moustache of cream over my top lip.

'Who's next?' she asked, eyes sweeping the room. Anna, used to Meena's constant attempts to alter her appearance, developed selective hearing and stood, back to the room, examining the books on Meena's shelf.

'How about you, Gillian?' Meena suggested.

Gillian raised one eyebrow. Which meant that the left-hand side of her monobrow was now slightly higher than the right.

'I'm not worried about upper lip hairs,' she said flatly.

'That wasn't what I was thinking,' Meena replied archly. 'I was thinking something slightly … higher?'

'My nose?' Gillian countered.

'No, higher still.'

'My fringe?'

'No…' Meena was struggling. She was clearly fixated

on the brow but didn't know how to bring it up. What reaction it might provoke. After all, she was dealing with St Mary's number one dick-kicker.

In the end Gillian herself came to the rescue. 'For God's sake, I know you're talking about my monobrow. I just wanted to see if you had the guts to mention it. And you didn't.'

'No,' murmured the gutless Meena. Gutless but not totally defeated. 'Have you ever thought about ... um ... er...'

'Just say it!'

'...plucking it?'

Me and Anna (who momentarily forgot to fake temporary deafness) both did a sudden intake of breath. Ducking slightly, waiting for the fire and fury. It didn't come.

'It doesn't bother me,' Gillian replied calmly. 'I've always had it.'

'But ... wouldn't you like to get rid of it?'

'I don't care,' Gillian repeated. 'But since you so clearly do – knock yourself out.'

'Does that mean...?'

'Yes. If it'll shut you up – tweezer me.'

Almost hopping from one foot to the other in glee, Meena sat Gillian at the end of her bed and again, almost as if by magic, produced a pair of bright pink tweezers. Where does she store this stuff? It's like she has a Mary Poppins-style make-up bag sewn into a secret pocket in her jeans.

'Right…' Meena said, 'I'm just going to take out the middle few. It might sting a little…'

'I'm not a baby,' huffed Gillian. 'I've been hit in the face by a hockey stick. I think I can handle tweezers.'

'Of course.'

Sure enough, Gillian's eyes didn't even water. Meena crouched down in front of her, her own brow furrowed in concentration. One hair from one side, one from the other.

She stood back to examine her work. Me and Anna joined her.

'What do you think?'

The monobrow was definitely no more. Two brows stood in its place. But something wasn't right. The symmetry was off.

'The left eyebrow starts closer in to the nose,' Anna proclaimed. 'Wait, I'll check.' She popped to Meena's desk and returned with a ruler. 'Taking the mid-point as the top of the nose… Gillian, is it OK if I mark it with a biro dot?'

Gillian nodded her assent and Anna duly dotted.

'…the start of the left eyebrow is two millimetres closer in than the start of the right eyebrow.'

'OK...' Meena plucked again at Gillian's left eyebrow. Anna came in with the ruler.

'Too much. The right eyebrow is now closer to the centre of the face.'

Meena was getting worried now. Her hands were starting to shake. The glint had disappeared from her eye. Normally I'd have been enjoying her discomfort but today I couldn't. My upper lip was starting to burn. As in, really sting.

'Meena—'

'Not now, India,' Meena snapped.

Anna was holding the ruler again. Meena's hands were shaking further. She swore. Meena very rarely swears. It was getting serious. I looked at Gillian's face and gasped. Meena had gone too far. In trying to balance up the brows, she'd plucked more and more so they were getting further and further apart. If she kept on going, Gillian would be left with a couple of eyebrow speech marks next to her ears. It was terrible. Truly terrible. I thought the monobrow was bad but at least it was Gillian. This was so much worse. Like those dogs that you sometimes see in photos where their owners have shaved and dyed their fur to make them look like other animals – lions, pandas etc, but they don't actually look like those animals they just look like weird mutant in-between species. Meena had created in-between Gillian.

'Um … all done!' declared Meena in a pitiful attempt at upbeat.

'Pass me the mirror,' Gillian commanded, pointing at the concave make-up one.

'Oh, NO … not that one,' Meena replied. 'The bathroom mirror's *much* better.' I knew for a fact that Meena's bathroom mirror's overhead light had been broken for a fortnight as she'd been moaning about this incessantly.

Gillian headed off to the bathroom. None of us dared follow.

'Meena, about my lip?' I asked again. The stinging was getting worse and worse. 'How long till I wash it off?'

'I don't know. I'm not timing it. I thought you were?'

'No I'm not. You're in charge, you're the one in charge!!!'

I raced to the bathroom to stand next to Gillian and splashed water over my mouth, again and again. The stinging died down slightly but the damage was done. Where there might once have been a few hairs was now a bright red moustache of irritated skin. 'Aggghhhhhh!' I screamed.

Me and Gillian returned to Meena's room together. Victims united.

'I look ridiculous,' Gillian said calmly. 'You're an idiot.'

'They'll grow back,' Meena grovelled. Deep down

she's terrified of Gillian. Terrified. 'I just googled to check. They'll definitely grow back.'

'And what about my face?' I spluttered far less calmly. 'What about when Rich sees this?'

'Oh calm down, India,' Meena barked. She's not scared of me. 'The redness will fade. It'll be fine in a couple of days.'

I left soon after.

Luckily Dad was already in bed when I got in.

Mum was annoyingly still up though and was halfway through her story about how Dad had hurt his back 'trying out a knee dive at the end of a chord' when she took one look at my face. She stopped talking, opened her mouth and then managed not to say anything else – sometimes she can be good like that. As I was brushing my teeth she put a little bottle of aloe vera gel on the windowsill next to me. It was almost like we were having a mother and daughter moment from a movie.

'You've got sensitive skin like me. Put a bit on and it'll calm down. Don't mess with your face, OK. You're beautiful as you are.'

I was right, it was a moment. We were definitely having a moment.

'Oh, and as you're sensitive you might want to think about showering with Femfresh like I do.'

And moment gone.

30th December.

We've got new neighbours. Well not *neighbour* neighbours, they're across the street from us rather than next door. I've had a lot of opportunity to check them out as my bedroom window looks straight into their front garden and front bedroom and I also get a pretty good view through their landing window too. The parents are a bit older than mine and Dad thinks they seem really shady as they smile the whole time. Moving furniture in – smiling. Carrying furniture up the stairs when they think no one can see – still smiling.

'Unnatural,' Dad said.

They even brought round a mini muffin basket as a 'get-to-know-you' gift.

'Who does that?? It's like they've read a manual on how to be a neighbour,' Dad spluttered.

I didn't go down to meet them. I pretended not to hear Mum calling repeatedly. Mainly because the skin above my mouth is still pretty red so I'm not ready for close-up viewings yet.

'What do you reckon, Samantha?' Dad asked as we were standing in the kitchen after they'd left.

'They seem very nice, Andrew.'

'Suspiciously nice,' Dad added. 'India, your mum can be very naïve sometimes. I'll tell you what I reckon … wait a moment…' Dad turned on the tap, muttering something like 'they're probably listening'. '… Undercover Russian spies. It's written all over them. You just need to be able to read the signs.'

I rolled my eyes. Dad's watching *The Americans* at the moment and is very easily influenced.

'I think it's very unlikely, Andrew,' Mum sighed.

'Don't think for one moment the Cold War is over,' Dad said, shaking his head. 'It's just gone underground. I'll watch the parents. India, you keep an eye on the kids. We won't have another Salisbury under my watch.'

'So when they slip up we call M15?' I asked sarcastically.

'Exactly,' he said, deadly serious. 'Here's a notebook.'

He thrust a small wirebound notebook into my hands with a slot for a pen on the top. It was actually pretty cool.

The 'kids' are both boys: a son called Pete who's about ten and then Dave, who's about eighteen and has a brooding look and far too good cheekbones to be British – maybe Dad does have a point after all.

'Dave and Pete – they're very British names,' Mum said, seeing Dad peeping out from behind the living room curtains, holding his bird-watching binoculars.

'Of course,' Dad said. 'Far too obviously British if you ask me. Their first rookie mistake.'

Mum rolled her eyes in my direction.

Dad always goes a bit mad over the Christmas period. Time off work doesn't suit him.

Later this afternoon as I sat in my room I saw the younger boy, Pete, staring up at me from their drive. He has such a round face, big eyes and small, freckled nose that he looks like a picture book child. I waved hello, good friendly neighbour (whose reporter's notebook just happened to be open). He didn't wave back. He winked. As in turned his head to one side slightly, smiled confidently, and winked. Oh my God. I think he's into me. I think a ten-year-old child is into me. And seems to think he has a chance.

I'm insulted. Horrendously insulted. And I need to upgrade to blackout blinds.

New Year's Eve.

Mum had the decency to leave me to sleep in till nine, but then was on top of me all morning.

'Have you made your bed yet?' she yelled up the stairs as I was pulling on my jeans.

'I'm still getting dressed!' I yelled back.

'Make your bed first!'

'I just want to put my jeans on.'

'Do you want to be successful or not?'

Me making my bed first thing is Mum's new obsession. Through her Article Club, she's read this piece about how all successful business people have one thing in common – they made their bed as a child – and now Mum seems to think I'll end up stacking shelves in Tesco for the rest of my life if I don't pull up and straighten my duvet every morning. I think the article's rubbish. Or at least it's drawn the wrong conclusion. One of those causation versus correlation things that school's always going on about. Maybe those people weren't successful because they made their beds. They were successful because they were motivated to leave home early to get away from overbearing parents shouting at them all the time.

'And have you done any more revision?'

'Yes!' I shouted back.

A lie.

I hadn't done any more. Having mastered the electromagnetic spectrum (I shared the RMIVUXG mnemonic with the gang and they were all very impressed) I kind of let everything else slide. As I said, priorities, priorities. These aren't even mocks. They are like mocks for mocks for mocks. Irrelevant. I've decided just to wing it. I'll probably remember most of the stuff anyway.

After a morning of mooching around the house I was bored so pretty pleased when my phone beeped with a message from Rich.

'Miss you. Can I Skype you at midnight?'

He seemed to have forgotten about my lack of smart phone.

But that didn't matter. What mattered was that he wanted to see me. I had a boyfriend who wanted to see my face at midnight on New Year's Eve. Even though I wouldn't be actually snogging a boy as Big Ben chimed, I was still getting one step closer.

I read his message again. I wanted to see him too. I really missed his crinkly eyes. His smile. His dimples. Even his forehead.

'I'll borrow Meena's phone,' I replied, giving him her number.

'Cool J x'

Putting my phone down I had a terrible thought and my hand flew to my mouth. I headed to the bathroom mirror. I couldn't let Rich see me with my weird red moustache. That would be a disaster.

I turned up the ceiling spotlights to max and switched on the extra mirror side lights. This wasn't a moment for flattering mood lighting. I needed to check this out properly. Like a scientist. Right … still redness in the upper lip area, but it had definitely faded. Nothing that some quite thick foundation couldn't handle. I tried a few more angles. No spots, excellent. No weird burst vessels in my eyes. My mole wasn't getting bigger. Hair was a bit limp and greasy but that was easy enough to fix. All was well in the world. Phew. Phewdy phew.

In the afternoon I took a shower, washed my hair and then mainly just sat around. It was still raining out and I knew I was going to be up really late so I had to conserve energy. Mum and Dad were lazing too. They were going round to their friends' on the street tonight and they always get really drunk and then are terribly hungover on New Year's Day even though they pretend not to be.

I headed to Anna's just after six. I'd put on a decent amount of foundation plus mascara and a tiny bit of bronzer and packed the make-up in a wash bag to take with me alongside my overnight stuff in case I needed to top up later. Pizza often requires some mouth wiping afterwards which could mean cover-up job ruined before you can say 'extra pepperoni'.

Grabbing my coat, I double-checked the results in the hall mirror. All still OK. I was camera-phone ready. Mum stopped me as I was leaving the house.

'Are you wearing make-up?'

'Have a good night too,' I replied sarcastically.

'Trust me, you need to let your skin *breathe*, India. To *heal*,' she added. 'You're only seeing friends. They won't care what you look like.'

I hadn't told her about the upcoming Rich video call. Obviously.

'It's just a bit of foundation, Mum. I've got to walk to Anna's. Along the streets. In public. I might *see* someone. Someone might *see* me.'

'No, India. This is for your own good. It's non-negotiable. You're not going anywhere till you wash that stuff off your face.'

Aggghhh.

Her hands were on her hips which meant her mind was set and there was nothing I could do to change it.

'Fine!' I yelled and ran up to the bathroom. Maybe it wasn't a big deal. It was dark out and I could put it on again as soon as I got to Meena's.

I stomped back downstairs, red moustached and unfriendly.

'Happy New Year, love,' Mum said as I headed out the door.

I grunted something that could have been interpreted as Happy New Year in return.

I was halfway down the front drive when Dad sprinted after me.

'There are definitely no boys at this party, are there?'

'Dad, it's not a party. It's a sleepover.'

'And there are no *boys* at this sleepover?' Dad's voice was rising up the octaves. 'Not, what's his name, the pervert?'

'You know perfectly well that his name is Rich. And, no, he's not coming. And, no, he's not a pervert. He's my "wonderful new boyfriend", remember?'

'He might turn up later.'

'He's still in Wales, he doesn't know where Anna lives, and Anna's parents are going to be there, downstairs, the whole time.'

'Hmmm.'

Finally satisfied, Dad wished me Happy New Year too and then padded back inside.

As I walked to Anna's along the High Street I passed Ennis and Anthony, clearly on their way to some uber-cool party or other. My hand flew to my face and I walked past them like I had some weird mouth-covering obsession. Ennis threw an 'Oh my God' glance at me and looked as if he thought he'd dodged a bullet.

The start of the night was brilliant.

We'd been worried Gillian might not show in protest at Meena's ruining her face, but she was there all right, arriving on the doorstep at the exact same time as me, perfectly friendly. I smiled 'hello' and then took a step back in shock. I literally couldn't believe it. It seemed scientifically impossible.

Gillian's monobrow was back.

After I'd got home that night I'd double-checked eyebrow regrowth on the home computer and Meena hadn't been lying when she said that plucked eyebrows grew back – what she hadn't said though is that it can take SIX MONTHS.

This had taken TWO DAYS. It wasn't yet as thick as before, but still – the speech mark effect was gone and in their place thinner brows that … met in the middle. It was like some superpower. A pretty rubbish superpower, but a superpower none the less. They should do experiments on her – maybe Gillian's genes could hold the cure to reversing baldness.

(Just to be clear, I don't mean lock-her-up-in-a cell type terrible experiments like they did on Wolverine. I'm thinking more like a nice lab where they offer you refreshments and you come and go very much on an outpatient basis. She could even cycle there.)

Anna opened the door and Meena stood beside her, looking sheepish. I'd been meaning to stay angry at her for longer, but she looked so down that I gave her a quick hug and Gillian slapped her on the back and everything was OK again. I went to the bathroom to reapply my make-up while the others ordered the pizzas – two extra pepperoni (for me and Anna), one ham and mushroom (for Gillian) and one ham and pineapple (for Meena). I can't believe Meena always chooses it. It's disgusting. The sweetness does not go. It does not 'compliment the savoury'. It's like spreading a bit of pudding on your main course. *The chicken with chocolate brownie for me, thanks.*

Next, we had to pick the films. We always watch two – one old, one new – as a sort of old year/new year thing. For the old one Anna had already chosen *Sleeping with the Enemy* – apparently a classic from the 90s. It sounded a bit rubbish but Anna was really excited. 'My mum says it's really good,' she said – as if that was actually a good thing. For the new one Meena insisted we watched *To All the Boys I've Loved Before*. I wasn't that keen but she'd read the book and said it was amaaaazing and so romantic.

Turns out Anna's mum has much better taste in movies than my best friend. *Sleeping with the Enemy* was excellent. I didn't quite get why Julia Roberts would have ever married the psycho with the towel-straightening obsession in the first place, or why she ended up with the weird looking guy leaping round the garden with a hose, but apart from that it was super-exciting. I'll never look at towels the same way again. The other film was really boring though. Don't write romantic letters to boys that you're not planning to send. Don't write letters to boys full stop. We had to pause halfway through so me and Meena could argue this one out and then, mid-argument, Meena's phone beeped. She looked at it and then passed it to me with an, 'It's for you.'

I read the text.

'Hey India, just thought I should tell you that I might look a bit different when I call. Didn't want to freak you out x'

Then there was a photo. Of Rich's face. I stared at it. He looked … exactly the same.

Hmmm. This was obviously not something I could solve alone.

'I'm pretty good at spot the difference,' Anna volunteered. 'Do you have another photo of him from before?'

I shook my head.

'You should always carry a photo of your boyfriend,' Meena reprimanded me.

'Why?' I asked.

'So you remember what he looks like.'

'I know what he looks like.'

'So why are we having this problem then?'

I stared at Meena's phone again. It didn't look like he'd had a haircut – maybe the curls were fractionally shorter at the front? I couldn't really see what he was wearing – maybe a dark T-shirt – but surely he didn't expect me to have memorised his entire wardrobe or be phased by a change in T-shirt colour?

I was stumped. Bamboozled.

'What shall I say?' I asked the gang.

Everyone agreed hair was the safest option.

'Nice haircut x' I texted back.

We waited, holding our breath.

'Haven't cut my hair,' came the reply.

Damn.

Another five second wait before his next text arrived.

'I know you're messing with me. Do you like the beard?'

Gillian was the first to break the silence.

'Beard? What beard?'

We all peered at the picture. No. Nothing.

'I'll get a magnifying glass,' said Anna.

Sometimes it's great to have a really practical friend who has a magnifying glass in their top drawer.

'Right…'

Anna held the lens over the phone and the lower half

of Rich's face tripled in size. Up close you could just about see them – what must have been only eight or nine hairs sprouting out of his chin. Rich's beard.

Oh God. It was horrible. Nothing-y, but horrible nonetheless.

'What are you going to say?' asked Gillian, genuinely interested.

'Love it x' I texted back.

'Don't worry, they'll make him shave it off for school,' Meena commiserated.

Thank God for school.

We ate ice cream after the pizza and I was just finishing wiping my mouth when I saw the time – 11:40pm. God. Rich would be calling any moment. Grabbing my make-up bag, I raced to the bathroom to patch up my foundation. I had just finished when Meena came in carrying her phone. Rich's face was on the screen. This time moving.

He started talking to me and I forgot all about his ridiculous 'beard'. I sat down on the bathroom floor and we talked and talked. He seemed so happy to see me and had so much to tell me about his Christmas and his cousins and I found I wanted to tell him all about my family too. I never normally tell people about my family.

'It's one minute to midnight,' he said, mid-flow. 'I… I…'

'Yes?'

'I thought maybe we could kiss phones at midnight and then it'd be like I was there, kissing you? Sorry – forget it, it's a stupid idea.' Rich's face was flushed bright red.

'No it's not,' I said. 'It's … romantic.'

Rich's dimples deepened.

'Ten,' came the shout from Meena's room.

'Nine.'

Rich started to lean towards his screen.

'Eight.'

I started to lean towards mine.

'Seven.'

Rich closed his eyes.

'Six.'

I decided to leave mine open. I always close my eyes when we kiss and this time I wanted to see his face.

'Five.'

He came closer.

'Four.'

I could see his eight/nine chin hairs now.

'Three.'

His mouth seemed abnormally large, distorted by the camera lens.

'Two.'

He tilted his face slightly more and I could see up his nostrils. Quite clearly up his nostrils.

'One.'

His mouth hit the screen, crumpling up his face and I decided that from now on I am only ever going to kiss boys with my eyes closed.

'Happy New Year!' he said, grinning, as he pulled away from the screen, nostrils shrinking back to normal size, their contents once again a mystery.

'Happy New Year!' I smiled back.

'I'm excited about spending this year with you,' he said sheepishly.

'Me too,' I replied.

And I meant it.

New Year's Day.

When I got home just after eleven, I found Mum and Dad sat in the kitchen, clearly feeling rough. They must have just got out of bed as they were still hunched over in dressing gowns. The lights were on the lowest setting, both were cradling mugs of coffee, their eyes were narrow slits and Mum kept on saying, completely unnecessarily, that they'd been 'up for hours'. I bet if I'd snuck upstairs their bed wouldn't even have been made.

New Year's Day tradition demands that we always go on a 'family walk' to 'blow the cobwebs away' so that was what we were going to do, regardless of the fact that none of us really wanted to. Mum and Dad were both in sunglasses even though it was completely overcast. Dad had originally planned to drive us further out into the countryside but when I'd very sensibly questioned whether he was 'OK to drive' Dad had exploded with a, 'Don't be ridiculous, India!' followed by a sheepish, 'Maybe it's best that we walk from the house.'

We reached the bottom of the hill that I normally complain about climbing and Dad looked at me with (what I imagine behind his shades were) pleading eyes.

'India, would you like us to turn back now?' he half-begged. 'I don't want you moaning all the way up.'

I smiled back at him. 'I'm feeling fine, thanks, Dad. Let's do it!'

I led the way and they followed after, panting with effort. This must be what really fit people feel like all the time. Soaring ahead with the riff-raff struggling behind. Being really fit must be awesome.

At the top of the hill there's this little van café where they sell bacon and sausage baps. It proudly displays its two star hygiene rating and Mum's always said in her most judge-y voice, 'Anyone who eats there is simply asking to get food poisoning.' This time, however, she strode straight up to it and ordered two more coffees and two double bacon baps.

'Oh sorry, did you want anything, India?' she asked as she returned, balancing cups and parcels of grease.

'No thanks, Mum. I've just always felt that anyone who eats there is simply asking to get food poisoning.'

Looking slightly less pallid after a heavy dose of nitrates (and probably salmonella), Mum asked about my night and I gave her a slightly edited version.

'Oh, I love *Sleeping with the Enemy* – so exciting. And the towels! Andrew, do you remember it?'

'What?' Dad's going deaf again. He can't have trimmed his ear hair for a while.

'*Sleeping with the Enemy*?' Mum repeated.

'Don't remember it.'

'You know, the one with Julia Roberts.'

Still nothing.

'The towels?'

'Oh yes – the towels! – great film.'

It must be really weird for some old movie star like Julia Roberts to have been in a hit film and have no one remember anything about it other than the rearrangement of a trio of towels.

'And did you speak to Rich at all?' Mum continued, mock-innocently.

I paused. I was about to say 'no' – it was none of

their business after all – but then I figured Rich might be around for a while so I had to at least be honest about his existence.

'Yes, a bit,' I said.

'It seems quite serious between you two,' she remarked.

I squirmed and Dad veered off the path.

We walked in silence for another ten minutes, Dad still keeping his distance slightly. Mum was clearly hatching a plan as her head was slightly on one side which is what happens when she's thinking deeply.

'Andrew,' Mum declared eventually. 'I think we'd better finally do what I suggested after Hope's and have India's boyfriend round for dinner. It's time we got to know him properly.'

There was a spluttering sound and I couldn't tell if it was coming from me or Dad.

I think it was coming from both of us.

When we got home, Mum immediately reached for the kitchen calendar.

'Right … when is Rich back from Wales?'

'Friday,' I said quietly.

'OK. Rich is back Friday… I've got Article Club on Friday Evening … Dad's auditioning for a band on Saturday … school starts on Monday.

'What?'

'Monday, India. School starts on Monday.'

'No, not that. What about Dad and a band?!?'

'Samantha, I told you not to tell her,' Dad hissed.

'It's fine. Dad misses playing, that's all. He's auditioning for a local band. It's good to have a hobby.'

'It's not just a hobby,' said Dad sulkily. 'Music has always been part of me. You can never take art out of the artist.'

Me and Mum rolled our eyes.

'So that leaves Sunday. It's settled. Invite Rich round for dinner here on Sunday night.'

I knew it was futile to resist. It looked like Rich was going to be around for a while which meant that at some point he was going to have to meet my parents. Maybe it was better just to get it over and done with. Ripping off plasters and all that.

I texted Rich later from my room.

'Oh, OK, great J!' came the reply. I didn't need FaceTime to tell that his face wasn't really smiling.

Saturday.

'Can I see you? xx Now?'

I got out of my post-breakfast shower to see this

really sweet text from Rich. He'd only just got back from Wales, he was already seeing me tomorrow night, but he wanted to see me sooner. Now.

'Sure, where?'

'The Green? 10?'

My heart sank a little. The *Green*. Boys always wanted to go to the Green. Images flashed before me of Yan suggesting we lie down behind the benches, of Ennis gnawing at my neck on a picnic rug before suffering a horrific reaction to my perfume and being bundled into an ambulance.

So far Rich had been different to all the boys I'd met before. Funny, kind, really easy to talk to. Not the sort of guy who wanted to 'go to the Green'. I hoped that wasn't all about to change.

Mum and Dad were fine about me going out – to be fair I just mumbled something about 'meeting the guys' so they didn't really know I was seeing Rich.

Rich was there before me – sat on a bench. He stood up as I approached, a massive grin almost splitting his face in two. I love the fact that he never plays it cool.

'Hey,' he said, the grin still intact.

'Hey,' I replied, feeling the corners of my mouth stretched to max.

Then he leant in and kissed me and I kissed him back. I shut my eyes the whole time and it was perfect.

'I shaved it off,' he said as we broke apart.

I must have looked as confused as I felt.

'My beard,' he explained. 'I got the feeling you weren't the biggest fan.'

'Oh, um … no … yeah,' I replied eloquently.

'And sorry about meeting here,' he said. 'I just wanted to be somewhere I could put my arm round you and kiss you without people staring.'

Somehow it didn't seem seedy when Rich said it. Choice of location forgiven.

I kissed him again.

'Right, down to business,' he declared.

I did my quizzical face.

'So I'm meeting your parents tomorrow night…'

My stomach triple jumped just hearing him say the words.

'And I need to impress them. I get the feeling that your dad doesn't like me very much.'

'No…' *pervert*. 'Not at all…' *that pervert*. I was trying to sound sincere but totally failed.

'Don't worry, India. I have a plan,' Rich said, suddenly looking very earnest and intelligent. Like a scientist making a breakthrough in a disaster movie. Or an architect. Pretty sexy, actually. I gave him another quick kiss.

'I watched a documentary the other day about how

to do well in interviews. Basically the candidates that succeed are the ones that mirror the interests and behaviour of the interviewer and thereby forge a subtle, psychological connection with them. I figured that meeting your parents is basically like an interview. So all I need is a comprehensive list of their interests and behavioural traits and then I can prepare to be the ideal candidate.'

'Right,' I said seriously. It did sort of make sense.

'Let's start with your mum. Any details, even the smallest, could be really helpful.'

I listed everything I could think of while Rich made notes.

- Works in marketing.
- Drinks flat whites.
- Likes active wear.
- Reads lots of articles.
- Is easily influenced by content of said articles.
- Weirdly obsessed with bed making.
- Says PLAHstic and ELAHstic as she thinks that's what posh people say.
- Thinks that she's into the environment and vegan food.
- Likes baking and makes inappropriate baking metaphors.
- Hates smart phones.

- Likes mindful colouring and embroidery.
- Expects her husband to destroy France to save her.

Rich nodded as he wrote these down, but I could tell by the gradual tightening of his pencil grip that he was getting more and more freaked out by the idea of my family. And that was just my mum.

'And your dad?' he squeaked.

- Is a dentist.
- Hates boys.
- Used to be in a band.
- Still thinks of himself as someone in a band.
- Is going to join a new band.
- Plays with adult Lego.

'Does that help?' I asked.

Rich's left knee was now shaking.

'I'm not sure,' he replied. 'But at least it gives me something to work with.'

Sunday morning. The day I'd hoped would never come.

It didn't start well.

I woke up early and began on my plan of being absurdly helpful around the house to get everyone in a good mood for tonight. As soon as I was out of bed, I made it, plumping up the pillow and everything. I even put the kitchen bin out, only to be greeted by Pete-the-child from across the road who was sat on his bike outside our house as if he'd been waiting for me like a stalker.

His eyes lit up as he saw me – unwashed hair in dressing gown. Wow. He must be really into me.

'Hi, India,' he said, giving me one of his face-to-one-side winks. 'Can I give you a lift somewhere?' He nodded to the back of his bike as if he was offering me a ride on his Harley rather than a backie on a bike that looked like the stabilisers had only just been removed.

'Um … I'm OK, thanks,' I said.

'Next time, then,' he said and pedalled off, turning back to look at me one … two … three times.

Dear God.

When I got back inside, Dad was stomping round the kitchen, clearly in a terrible mood.

'Where's the Nescafé, Sam?' he barked. 'I can't find the Nescafé.'

'It's in the cupboard, Andy,' Mum replied calmly. 'Where it always is.'

'No, that jar's empty.'

'Well, I'll buy some more later then. Why don't I make you a Nespresso for now?'

'I don't drink Nespresso. There's nothing wrong with Nescafé. Why are people always trying to change things? There's nothing wrong with the old stuff. Nothing!'

Dad stormed out of the kitchen and Mum didn't even shout at him. I got the feeling that this wasn't really about coffee.

Mum came over. All quiet and super-tactful, clearly enjoying her self-appointed role of understanding peacemaker.

'Be nice to your dad this morning. He had a bit of a blow last night.'

'What?' I asked.

'The band he auditioned for. They turned him down. Said his playing and choice of songs was too "retro" for them. That they were looking for a "fresher" sound.'

Oh no. Dad would be gutted. Angry and upset. Not the state I wanted him in to meet Rich. Tonight was going to be even worse than I'd thought. I debated packing a bag and running away then and there. I wondered whether it was still possible to hitch-hike and, if so, what the percentage chance of being murdered was. Probably not much over 25%.

The day dragged and dragged. I offered to go down the shops and get Dad some more Nescafé. I even offered to help tidy up his Lego and volunteered out of nowhere that *Born to Run* was a classic that should be appreciated by every upcoming generation.

In response I got: 'Mum's already been', 'Don't touch my Lego' and 'Are you mocking me now?'

So I stayed away, instead helping Mum get ready for dinner (including persuading her that beef lasagne might go down better than her normal three bean version). I even cleaned the bathroom. I figured if Dad was going to be horrific then I needed Mum as much on side as possible.

Finally 7:30pm came round and there was a knock on the door.

I rushed to open it.

'Hey,' Rich stammered, his smile frozen on his face. 'How's it going?'

'Ummm… Fine. *Fine*.' That told him everything he needed to know. I saw that he was considering risking the 25% chance of death by hitch-hiking too, so I dragged him inside and shut the door before he could flee.

'Richard!' Mum cooed, bustling into the hall. 'So lovely to finally meet you!'

Rich took baby steps inside.

Dad, standing behind her, grunted.

Richard took a deep breath in and gave his hands a tiny little shake, like an actor getting into character.

'Good evening, Mr and Mrs Smythe,' he said. 'I brought these flowers.' He thrust a bunch of tulips into Mum's hands. 'I hope you don't mind,' he continued, 'but I insisted on no *PLAH*stic wrapping as it's so damaging for the environment.'

My mouth dropped opened. He was doing it. Operation mirroring was a go. Surely he couldn't be so blatant and get away with it? I watched Mum's face. She was beaming. Positively beaming. It was working. It was actually working!

Then I looked at Dad. Turns out the copy-the-interviewer technique works best when there's only one interviewer. Dad was turning red and making some weird spluttering sounds. I could tell he was torn. He thought Rich was taking the piss out of Mum's pronunciation of plastic, but he couldn't say anything without acknowledging that Mum sounds ridiculous, a fact he's buried his head in the sand about for the last fourteen-plus years.

'Come through to the living room,' Mum said, ushering us right.

'Have you had a nice day?' Mum asked Rich.

'Yes, lovely, thank you. I made my bed first thing, *of course*, and then did a bit of baking. Baking really soothes my mood, if you know what I mean?'

'I do, I do,' said Mum, earnestly.

'If I've had a bit of a bad day, it lifts my spirits like a well-risen soufflé.'

Too much, Rich, too much. Rein it in!

Dad was glaring daggers at him. But apparently it wasn't too much for Mum. She'd found her new best friend.

Rich, sensing that he was only playing to one side of the room, turned to Dad and said, 'Well, when I'm not doing Lego, of course.'

'Hmmmpphhh,' Dad snorted.

'I've got a new set,' Rich persevered. 'I don't know if you know the Creator Expert series?'

'Of course I do.'

'Well, I've started on the London Bus.'

'Have you now?' Despite himself, Dad's interest was beginning to be piqued. 'How many pieces is that?'

'1686. Special elements include a new for August 2017 tyre with standard tread and reversible transit advertising posters.'

'Right, right.'

I had to hand it to Rich. When he researches, he doesn't cut corners.

The timer went off in the kitchen.

'Lasagne's ready!' cried Mum, grabbing Rich by the arm.

I overheard him offer to send her a recipe for his roast veg vegan version as we walked through.

He was truly on fire.

After we'd finished the lasagne – 'Delicious, Mrs Smythe, thank you' – 'Please call me Samantha' – Rich brought the talk round to music and I tensed up. This was not going to go well.

'Mr Smythe, India mentioned that you're joining a band?'

Silence.

'What sort of band is it?'

Shut up, Rich. Read the room and shut up!

'It didn't work out in the end,' Dad replied cagily. 'They thought it'd be difficult having a more experienced front man. You could say they were jealous.'

Could, if you were a total liar.

'And I respect their decision. Jealously is bad for a band. It's what tears it apart.'

Dad was intentionally not catching Mum's eye. Meanwhile Rich was nodding his head vigorously in agreement.

'Yes, totally. That's why there's no front man in my band. It's me and my cousins – completely equal. We each take turns to sing.'

'What do you play?' Dad was interested. He was actually interested.

'All sorts. That's the great thing about the cello, oboe, flute combination. It's so versatile.'

Dad looked at him like he must have misheard.

'Sorry – for a moment there I thought you said cello, oboe and flute?'

'Yes – I did!'

A derisive snort erupted from Dad's nose.

'Play me some,' he commanded.

'No!' I interjected. I didn't want Rich subjected to Dad's ridicule. 'There's no need.'

'It's not up to you,' Dad snapped.

'It's fine, India,' Rich reassured me. 'I've got a bit recorded on my phone.'

He pulled out his iPhone and Mum rolled her eyes. India's boyfriend was a *smart phone user*. It was all going downhill.

Rich scrolled through. 'Here … no, not that one … this one … yup, this one's probably best…'

He pressed play.

I fought the urge to hide under the table.

And then … I actually listened and realised something. It was good. The music was actually good. It had a great beat, a soulful tune over the top, a catchy chorus. It must have been one of Rich's cousins singing as I didn't recognise the voice. But overall … really, surprisingly, good.

I watched for Dad's reaction.

'Not … bad…' he said slowly. 'Not bad at all…'

Mum, Rich and me all breathed a sigh of relief.

'It needs something though … something's missing…'
Dad began scratching his chin in the worst ever
impression of a man thinking. He had a plan. Oh God,
Dad had a plan. '…that's it – guitar! It needs a backing
guitar. Some sweet chords to give it depth and texture.
Follow me to the garage, young man.'

Rich looked at me with deer-in-the-headlight eyes.

'Maybe you should let Rich have his dessert first?'
Mum suggested. 'I've made Bakewell tart.'

'Nonsense. This is more important. Rich, are you
coming?'

He had no choice and I couldn't save him.

Rich followed my dad out to the garage and me and
Mum sat in silence for the next forty minutes as we heard
Dad amp up his guitar and riff over Rich's recording.

Finally the noise stopped and Dad and a very ashen-
faced Rich reappeared. Dad was beaming. Rich's left
knee was shaking.

'Great news!' Rich said in a wavering voice. 'Your
Dad's decided to join my band!'

6th January – school starts again.

Some people are always really pleased to get back

to school after the holidays. Me, not so much. Obviously, it's good to get away from my parents, but they're back at work today anyway so that becomes less of a motivator. Plus we've got days of tests to welcome us back which is never fun.

I met the gang by the entrance so we could all walk in together.

'How's band practice going?' sniggered Meena.

'Ha ha,' I sarcastically laughed back, wishing I'd never told her. Meena thinks my Dad forcing his way into Rich's band is the funniest thing that has ever happened. Thank God Rich's cousins live in Wales and only visit about twice a year. Rather limits potential rehearsal time.

'Right,' said Anna, tactfully trying to change the subject. 'Who wants to quickly go over Physics?'

Meena frowned hard – a caricature of concentration. Physics isn't really her thing. Screwing up her nose for extra thinking power, she managed to come out with: 'Radio waves, Microwaves, Infrared, Visible light, Ultraviolet, X-rays, Gamma rays,' and then semi-collapsed from effort.

'Amazing!' declared Anna, amazed.

'Rachel's Mum Is Very Ugly X Gillian,' cried Meena, high-fiving me. Seems I might have made up the best mnemonic device ever!

After an excruciatingly boring assembly about being 'the best possible versions of ourselves', we were on our way to the science lab for our Physics test when all around me I started to hear whispered snippets of conversation. 'Rachel's Mum' ... 'Very Ugly' ... 'Gillian' ...

'What's going on?' I hissed at Meena.

'Oh, I may have told a few people about your thing,' she said airily. 'Don't worry, I didn't tell Rachel.'

'But ... but,' I was seized by a moment of panic. 'It'd be OK if she found out, wouldn't it? I mean Rachel's mum's obviously really beautiful so she wouldn't mind, would she?'

Meena gave me a strange look.

'Everyone can be beautiful on the inside,' she replied.

I didn't get it. I didn't get it at all, but there was no time to ask more questions. Ms Frammel was ushering us into the lab. Question papers had already been laid out on benches and I was starting to get that knot in my stomach that exams, however trivial, always give me.

The test didn't go well. I think I got all the electromagnetic spectrum stuff right but I hadn't revised kinetic and gravitational potential energy calculations and it turns out you can't really wing those.

'How did it go?' Gillian asked as we walked down the corridor towards French.

'Pretty well,' said Anna.

'Good for you,' declared Gillian. 'I hate it when girls put themselves down and say it went badly when they know it was probably good. Boys don't do that.'

'How did you find it, Gillian?' I asked.

'Bad. I got about 35%. I'm not good at Physics and didn't revise. I'm not putting myself down. I'd get near 100% in a sports exam, but this school doesn't do them.'

Right. Logical appraisal. Good.

The French exam didn't go well either. It seems I'm not naturally gifted at languages. I'd watched a couple of episodes of a French Netflix show called *Call my Agent!* with Mum in the holidays and thought that sort of counted as my French revision. If only the exam had had subtitles.

I tried not to feel down as I got home. After all, I kept telling myself, these exams weren't important. They were at best indicators of what we needed to improve at. I'd revise hard before the actual GCSEs.

After dinner, I curled up on the sofa and texted Rich. I needed a bit of comfort.

'How's it going?'

'Can't talk now,' came the reply. 'Will explain later.' Then a pause, followed by a 'x'. An afterthought 'x'. That didn't bode well. I'd never got an afterthought 'x' before. All previous 'x's had definitely been main body of text 'x's.

My thoughts were interrupted by a clattering from the stairs and Dad came down carrying the desktop computer from the landing, dragging the plug and still-connected printer lead behind it. I peered round the living room door to see him heading out the side door to the garage.

'What's going on?' I asked.

'Band practice!' he called back. 'I realised our band wasn't going to get anywhere if we only rehearsed twice a year. Then it struck me – we don't have to rehearse in the same place. There's this great new app called Zoom. We'll all see each other on the screen in 'gallery mode' so it'll be like we're jamming side by side. Except we won't. We'll be in garages spread across Surrey and West Wales.

Oh God. Poor Rich.

No wonder I got an afterthought 'x'. The only time Dad decides to embrace technology, it's to ruin my life.

I've decided to get fit. Another day of particularly bad exams yesterday put me in a bit of a downer and exercise is meant to cheer you up. Endorphins and all that.

'What do you think?' I asked the gang.

'Not sure it's for you,' Meena replied.

'What rubbish!' declared Gillian. 'It's a great idea. And you're horrifically unfit.' *Thanks.* 'You've picked the perfect time to start. All the school sports clubs take on new members at the beginning of each term. You just have to pick one and sign up.'

Gillian dragged us all over to the lists that were pinned to the noticeboard outside the main hall. Even the noticeboard smelt of sweat and old trainers. I was starting to have second thoughts.

'So…' said Gillian, waving a hand in the direction of the lists. 'Pick one.'

'Will you sign up too?' I begged Meena and Anna.

'Sorry, I'm too busy with orchestra,' said Anna.

I turned to Meena.

'No,' said Meena.

I scanned the lists.

Hockey…? No, I hate hockey. And why increase my chances of being bashed in the face by a long wooden stick and ending up with a weird asymmetrical nose?

Swimming…? No, you have to go to the freezing-cold local pool twice a week after school and do about a million laps. I'd probably also have to learn butterfly. The most pointless stroke of all time.

Tennis …? No, I'm rubbish at tennis. I can't even serve. It would just be too embarrassing.

Cross-country …? Hahahahahahaha.

Netball…? *Netball?* That might be the way to go. It's not that tiring. I can catch a ball. I can throw a ball. I can remember which white lines I'm supposed to stay inside. As long as I'm not Goal Attack or Goal Shooter I wouldn't even need to be able to get the ball through the hoop.

I wrote my name on the list and Gillian patted me on the back.

'Good girl,' she said.

I checked when the first practice was – Thursday, as in tomorrow. OK. Right. I'll be ready…

I texted Rich as soon as I got home but got no reply so I just hung around the house watching Netflix while tokenly looking at History till Mum got home.

The first thing she asked as she got in was how today's tests had gone.

'Not the best,' I admitted and then regretted it as I watched her back tense and straighten, taking her to a five foot seven. I changed tack, 'But OK … yes, definitely OK.' Her back hunched over again, slightly.

'And I've joined Netball Club,' I added, still pretty proud of myself (and feeling quite a lot fitter already).

'Oh good!' she cried (and definitely meant it as her back relaxed enough to go full hunch).

'What are you making?' I asked. Mum was pulling on an apron and taking the scales and a bowl out of the cupboard. Always a good sign.

'Oh, tonight I thought I'd try out a little lemon soufflé recipe that Rich sent me. He said it's a good first step towards the Grand Marnier soufflé – the most challenging soufflé of all time!'

What?

Just then my phone beeped. It was Rich, finally. 'Hope you're OK. Just got back from orchestra and I've got band practice in five.'

With that, Dad's car revved up onto the drive. He waved at us through the kitchen window and headed straight for the garage. To jam with my boyfriend.

Right. That was it. Operation mirroring had gone too far.

Rich was spending far more time with my parents than with me. I was stuck in some horrific, incestuous foursome.

'No…' I growled. 'No…'

Mum watched me glaring at the garage door.

'I think it's nice,' she said. 'Girls always go for boys a bit like their dad.' *Agggggghhhhhhh*. 'But in your case, you've chosen someone a bit like your mum as well. I'm flattered.'

I'm not going to get any sleep tonight.

I actually slept like a baby – nine hours straight through. But it still didn't change the fact that I needed to break Rich and my parents up, and fast.

I arranged to meet him tonight after netball practice. My parents would never normally let me out after school on a Thursday, but this was the last day of tests and as soon as I said it was with Rich, they were all 'it's fine' as they're so into him.

Doing badly in today's tests didn't bother me as much. It was like I was used to not knowing the answers. *A-ha, my friends, ignorance and blank spaces, nice to see you again.*

Anyway, it meant I was still feeling reasonably positive after school when I followed Gillian to the changing rooms, munching my Monster Munch for energy as I went. Until I started to get undressed … and saw the other members of netball club arrive: members who included … April and Lisa. No. No. NO. I think they only joined to show off quite how good their absurdly long, flawless legs looked in a short skirt. Netball was the closest St Mary's got to cheerleading.

'Hello, India,' April purred dangerously. 'I'm surprised to see you here.'

'Yes,' Lisa echoed, 'netball's quite a delicate game. Wouldn't shot-put be more of your thing?'

Cue tinkling, evil laughter.

Gillian stood up and stepped in front of me.

'No more,' she said and they backed down. They actually backed down! It's like I'm friends with a pit bull. Or a member of the police. Don't mess with India Smythe – she's got back up. I could have hugged Gillian, but I knew she'd probably punch me so I didn't.

Then the final member arrived. Late. Rachel Turner.

I felt this sinking feeling come over me. I've felt really guilty about the mnemonic Physics thing ever since hearing it repeated around school. It wasn't meant to be mean. It wasn't about this Rachel, or any Rachel for that matter, and especially not her mum, but hearing it again and again wasn't making me feel the greatest. I wanted to mention it to her. To smooth things over. But I didn't know how to bring it up and she didn't look upset or anything. I don't think she was even aware there was anything to smooth. As Mum says, 'You don't iron a no-crease top.'

Right, I was ready to go. At least I thought I was.

'Aren't you forgetting something?' Gillian asked.

I thought for a moment. 'No.'

'Your tights?'

'What about them?'

'You can't play netball in tights.'

'But it's *freezing*. It's *January*.'

'Doesn't matter. No. Tights.'

'OK. I'll put on my joggers then.'

'No joggers!' said Gillian in disgust. 'Netball is played in a skirt. Full stop. Is nothing sacred to you?'

I wanted to say that's because it's normally a summer sport, but I saw the determined set of her face, the intensity of the now-even-bushier-than-before monobrow and realised there was no point resisting. I looked round the changing room. Everyone else had bare legs. No one else was complaining. This wasn't going to be an 'I am Spartacus' moment.

Joining Netball Club had been a terrible mistake.

I sat down on the bench and unpeeled my wonderfully thick, soft grey tights. To reveal … blindingly white legs that hadn't seen the sun for five months. It was like looking at sun bouncing off snow. If snow hadn't been shaved for a week. I winced at the sheer intensity of their paleness and April asked Lisa to 'pass me my shades'. Hilarious. Absolutely hilarious.

There was no time to attempt to crawl away and hide. With a sharp whistle blow to announce her arrival, Ms Hatchard, our PE teacher, sprang into the changing room. What an unnecessary entry. We know she has a whistle. It comes with the job. It's not like Miss Owen, our Maths teacher, bounds into the classroom with an outstretched protractor.

'Welcome, new arrivals!' she barked, bouncing up and down on the spot. Heaven forbid her heart rate dropped below a hundred and thirty for a second. 'Follow me!'

It was already dark on the netball court but the feeble floodlights had been switched on so we could just about see. The PTA are desperately raising money to try to upgrade them but the ideas they come up with are always so lame and inevitably involve the words St Mary's and the school crest being stamped onto random stuff. The St Mary's biro – £2 – five items sold. The St Mary's diary – £12 – three items sold. The St Mary's hoodie to wear at weekends (!?!?) – £20 – zero items sold.

My knees were knocking together from cold, a fact which, unfortunately, Ms Hatchard pounced on.

'India looks cold,' she yelled, despite the fact that we were all right next to her. She doesn't seem to be able to adjust volume. 'Let's warm her up. Ten laps everyone!'

Oh no. Ten laps of the court! And my fault. Everyone stared daggers at me apart from Gillian who whispered, 'Nice one!'

We set off. I wasn't at the back. I was in the middle. Maybe I wasn't so unfit after all. Three sides of the court completed, the leaders started cutting back. Ms Hatchard blew her whistle. 'Not the court!' she yelled. 'The whole tarmacked area.'

Oh God. There were three courts … that made … a big area. I had basically signed up for cross-country after all.

I wasn't in the middle of the pack for long. Seems that other people had been 'pacing themselves'. After the second lap I was firmly at the back with a pain in my side so bad I began to wonder if it was actually acute appendicitis. Gillian overtook me again.

By the time I'd finished, I was dripping with sweat, red in the face and my whole body hurt. I even took off my sweatshirt and put it on the side. That's how sadistic the whole thing was. No one should be choosing to be outside in just a T-shirt in January.

'Feel a bit warmer now?' Ms Hatchard crowed, blowing her whistle again for maximum effect.

I think I might hate Ms Hatchard.

She then split us into two teams and handed out bibs. I was in the red team: Goal Keeper. Good, I thought. I don't think that's a very important position. You just stick to the Goal Shooter and try to stop them scoring. And you can only move around one third of the court. It's almost like sitting down.

I was smiling to myself until I looked at the other team. There, with her impossibly long legs, in the yellow GS bib, stood April. No. NO. NO. I had to stick right next to April for the next ... *check watch* ... 32 minutes.

'In position, girls!' yelled Ms Hatchard.

April sashayed over and looked at me in disgust, wrinkling up her nose. 'Did you even put deodorant on?' she asked. My, 'Of course' was swallowed by the noise of the whistle. The ball started shooting around all over the place, much faster than normal school netball played by normal-level people. I was out of my depth. Completely out of my depth. Yellow team got the ball. It flew from WA to GA to GS. April. God. I had to do something. I had to at least look like I was trying to stop April score. I leapt around in front of her, arms outstretched, mouth open in effort.

April aimed at the goal. I leapt higher. The ball soared through the air and through the hoop.

Yellow bibs cheered. Red bibs groaned.

'Can't believe you're still eating Monster Munch,' April sneered. I can smell them from here... And you really need to shave under your arms.'

I didn't have a clever come back, but even if I'd had, there wouldn't have been any time to use it as the whistle blew again and the cycle was repeated, pretty much exactly the same as before.

'Defend, Goal Keeper, defend!'

The call took me by surprise – it wasn't Ms Hatchard's voice – and I swivelled round to see where it was coming from as April scored another goal.

'Eye on the ball!'

There it was again. Or rather there *she* was – Keen Mum. Stood behind the netting. Getting too involved in school sport. There was always one. I thought they only turned up to matches though, not to practices as well.

'Break!' called Ms Hatchard and we wandered to the side. I wondered what we'd get. A doughnut maybe? A KitKat? But no … it was a bowl of … *lift covering tea towel* … orange wedges. Orange wedges?! I'd run ten mega laps and leapt up and down and all I got was orange wedges?!

From the side of the court I could see Keen Mum up close. She was particularly horrific looking. A weaselly face with a sharp nose, pinched mouth and deep frown lines from years of vocal disapproval. Probably the most unattractive person I'd ever seen and I'm no beauty fascist. I think Roald Dahl got it about right in *The Twits* when he said something along the lines of anyone can look nice if they have nice thoughts. I mean Mrs Baker from the church has totally wonky features, a big nose and about four chins, but she's so smiley that you think 'what a nice woman'. Keen Mum, however, has probably never smiled in her whole life and it shows. My, it shows.

'Who's that?' I whispered to Gillian – nodding in the direction of Keen Mum.

'Oh, that's Rachel Turner's mum.'

W-h-a-t?

It was like the whole world stopped moving and was replaced by a dark, cavernous hole.

'It … can't … be,' I stammered. 'I've met Rachel's mum. A couple of times. At parents' evening. She's… she's really beautiful.'

'No,' Gillian replied slowly as if I was a complete moron. 'Rachel's *other* mum. She travels a lot so she misses most things. But she comes to practices and matches occasionally.'

Rachel's. Other. Mum.

It was so unfair! How could I have known? Rachel doesn't talk about it. Why should she, I guess? I don't exactly go around saying, 'I live with my biological mother and father. How about you?' And there are a hundred and fifty girls in the year. I can't know all the home life details of a hundred and fifty people!

Suddenly Meena's reaction to my 'Rachel's Mum is hot' comment all made sense. She'd known. So why hadn't she told me? Why the hell hadn't she told me?!

I was in a state of shock for the rest of the practice. Back in the changing rooms I even put my school uniform back on, completely forgetting that I'd brought normal clothes to change into, and set off home. Halfway up Hill Drive I got a text from Rich.

'You still coming?'

Damn. I'd totally forgotten. I was supposed to be meeting him in Rainston … *check watch* … now.

Agggggghhhh!

I ran back down the road and leapt on the next bus. Twenty minutes later I was outside the Fountain Centre where we said we'd meet. I caught sight of myself on the mirrored escalator sides as I rushed in the main entrance. Face still flushed, hair plastered to my face from sweat, bit of a stain on my school shirt from where the chutney had dropped out of my sandwich. Not a good look. I had to get to the toilets before he saw me. I swivelled right, but it was too late.

'India!'

Head down. Keep going. Pretend you haven't heard him.

'India!'

Damn.

There was the sound of running and then a tap on my shoulder.

'Oh, hi Rich, didn't see you there.'

He was standing there smiling, obviously not in school uniform, obviously not covered in sweat. Not a chutney stain in sight.

'You look … nice,' he attempted.

Then he burst out laughing and I couldn't help it, I burst out laughing too.

'Netball practice,' I kind of explained. 'Give me a minute.'

I ran into the toilets, changed into my jeans, splashed water on my face, tried to de-flatten my hair a little using the hand drier and put on some of the emergency foundation I carry in my bag in case of an unexpected spot.

I didn't look good, but I looked passable.

Rich was still grinning when I re-emerged.

'Glad you're finding this so funny,' I said.

'I just like you, that's all. I think I really like you.'

He put his arm round me and pulled out his phone. 'Smile!'

The photo wasn't the best. He must have exhaled at the last moment as his hair was shooting upwards lengthening his forehead and my mouth looked far too big and my cheeks were more hot-cross-bun doughy than chiselled cheek bones, but we both looked … happy. Really happy.

'Mind if I share it?' he asked awkwardly. 'It's just I've never had a hot girlfriend before.'

'That's fine,' I simpered. I hadn't realised how weak I am when it comes to flattery.

Psycho: Want to get in my car?

Me: No way.

Psycho: But you look so hot in a seat belt.

Me: Oh, OK then.

He posted the photo on Insta and there was an instant like. Not having a smart phone myself, it seemed pretty exciting. I kind of get why Mum thinks they're addictive. Not that I'd ever tell her that.

'Who is it?' I asked, trying to sound like I didn't really care. 'Who liked it?'

Rich looked.

'SSmythe74.'

My mum.

Rich looked at my downturned face.

'Sorry – your mum followed me a few days ago and I thought I had to accept.'

I nodded glumly.

'And, I should probably tell you, your Dad's invited me round for band practice on Sunday.'

'What are we going to do about them?' I asked.

'I don't know, I really don't know,' he replied in a small voice. 'I'd hoped they'd just sort of lose interest.'

'Me too.'

It wasn't the craziest thought. Mum's interests normally change from week to week. Dad's last longer though.

We were both looking super-down now.

'Come on, India,' Rich said eventually. 'Situations like these...' he began, but then we both burst out laughing. There weren't 'situations like these'. There might never have been a situation like this in the whole of humanity. This was a very unique, completely horrific one-off. '...Situations like these call for ice cream and bowling.'

So that's what we did and it was awesome.

Saturday.

I woke up with a brainwave.

I had a plan of how to deal with Mum. If I'm a victim to flattery, she's a victim to magazine articles. Every week a different article is laminated and stuck to the fridge with a huge wine-glass-shaped magnet. This week's had been on how regularly walking barefoot on grass could help 'realign your ionic flow'. It is the reason the stair runner still has traces of muddy footprint on it. Dad went ballistic when he first saw it.

Dad: India, what's this mess on the stairs?

Me: It was Mum, not me!

Dad: Samantha?!

Mum: Don't you even care about my ionic flow?

Dad: (*Thinking this might be some sort of period reference*) Errr…

The articles are normally ones she's been reading with her Article Club, but there was no reason they had to be.

I waited till Mum and Dad were having their half an hour regular weekend coffee slot at 9:30am and then turned on the landing computer.

Operation fake article was a go.

I googled a few articles first to get up to speed on style and pacing etc and conducted a bit of my own analysis.

Right, what the sample of ten articles all seemed to share was:

1   The title was a terrible pun

2   They included loads of outlandish and often unprovable claims to incense the reader

3   There was a quote from a total nobody

4   There was always some bit of dodgy basic psychology, and
5   There were often a few bullet points in a different font in a box.

OK. Twenty-one minutes of coffee break left – I had to get this done and fast.

Title first:

Stay Mum – or lose your daughter forever!

Pun: tick. I was on fire.

Now for the text.

Nowadays many mums are getting more and more involved in their daughters' lives, driven from a genuine desire to connect in a way they maybe hadn't with their own mothers. However, caution should be exercised. Whilst it is only natural for mums to want to share experiences with their daughters, there is one area they should leave well alone: their love life. Any attempt to bond too closely with their daughter's boyfriend or girlfriend is bound to end in disaster and push the daughter away so that she may, in extreme cases, never talk to her mother again.

I felt a bit guilty about this last sentence as I know Mum really wants to be close to me and do more stuff together. Then I remembered the recipe share. And the Instagram like.

I had to be brutal.

Jo from Kent says, 'I remember when I first invited my daughter's boyfriend over for dinner. Before I knew it I had texted and emailed him five times the following week. I had a problem and I sought help, but it was too late. I don't know where my daughter is now. She moved out the house. One of her friends mentioned she might have gone to Australia.

My Mum's biggest fear is that I move to Australia when I'm older. 'You'll be a day away,' she wails, 'and I'm terrible with jet lag.' Back to the article.

As Dr Elridge, a prominent but reclusive psychologist, writes, 'The mother's desire to insert herself into her daughter's relationship stems from a fear of losing her own biological appeal. It is based on Oedopus.' (Spell check) *'Oedipus.'*

I'm not totally sure what happened in Oedipus, but everything seems to be based on it.

Now time to change font.

Five crucial don'ts when it comes to your daughter's relationships:

Don't:

- Follow her boyfriend/girlfriend on Instagram
- Share recipes with her boyfriend/girlfriend
- Text her boyfriend/girlfriend
- Let your husband join her boyfriend/girlfriend's band

105

- Ask her boyfriend/girlfriend if she wants to join a club.

Mum texted Rich last night to see if he was interested in joining her Article Club 'because they have so many interests in common'. *Too far, Mother, too far.* Plus she's never asked me to join – I wouldn't want to, of course – but the point still stands.

I reread the article and felt pretty pleased with my efforts. I played with the fonts and layout for a while, settling on 'Cambria' for the main body and 'Arial' for the bullet points. Final touch was adding in a photo of a woman sitting, head in hands, with the caption, '*If only I'd kept my distance*'.

And print.

Game face on, I padded downstairs and sat at the kitchen table. The crucial thing was not to say anything. Just to sit there and pretend to be engrossed.

It only took three minutes.

'What are you reading, love?'

'Oh, just a really interesting article… Meena sent it to me. We're thinking of starting our own Article Club.'

'Oh? Right.'

Mum smiled.

'May I?'

'Sure, I've just finished it. It makes some really good

points,' I said gravely and then left the room as if deep in thought and slightly troubled.

Ten minutes later there was the sound of the front door slamming.

'Where's Mum gone?' I asked.

'Not quite sure,' Dad replied. 'But she said she'd be out for a while. Which means … we can have burgers for lunch!' Mum can't stand burgers but Dad keeps an emergency stash in the freezer for occasions such as these.

Around twelve while I was helping Dad assemble the burgers, I got a text from Rich to say Mum wasn't following him on Instagram any more and had messaged him to say that there weren't any spaces left in Article Club after all.

It was working. My ingenious plan was totally working!

I'm a manipulator extraordinaire.

I'm basically Machiavelli.

I wonder if Machiavelli ever made his mum cry.

Mum came back home around three. She had puffy eyes and an elongated back and didn't hang around in the house but went straight into the garden and pretended to look at the plants. I know she was pretending because it's January so everything's dead and 'looking at plants' basically entails staring at soil with a few sticks in it.

'What's up with Mum?' I asked Dad quietly.

'I don't know, love,' Dad replied. He even looked a bit worried. 'She said something about reading a fake article. She wouldn't get into it. You know what she's like about some things. She'll calm down by dinner.'

I was only half-listening to what he was saying. My attention broke off at the words 'fake article'. Oh. No. What had I done? I thought the article was really convincing. I wonder what gave it away? It's possible it was a little too specific...

Turns out I'm less Machiavelli, more terrible forger who gets thrown in jail for trying to pass off handwritten bank notes.

What's worse, I'd really upset Mum. She may be a pain and really embarrassing, but at the end of the day, she's my mum and I love her. I had to sort this out.

I pulled on a coat and headed out into the garden.

She was standing at the far end, pretending to be engrossed in the compost heap.

'Sorry, Mum,' I murmured.

She didn't say anything for a while, just kept staring at the ground.

Finally, she opened her mouth. 'I just don't understand why you couldn't talk to me? Why you felt you had to invent an *article* to tell me to stay away from Rich?'

'Ummm…'

When she put it like that it didn't seem like the greatest behaviour. But Mum isn't that easy to talk to. She can get mad sometimes. She's sensitive. She overreacts.

'I didn't think you'd take it so well,' I said.

'What do you mean? I'd take it fine,' her voice was rising.

'You nearly divorced Dad when he said he wouldn't destroy France for you.'

Mum snorted loudly.

'I'm sorry, Mum. It's just … he's my first boyfriend. And I kind of want to spend time with him. Alone. Just the two of us. And I'm worried you guys will frighten him away.'

'I'm not frightening!'

She wasn't listening. She wasn't listening at all. I had to appeal to her vanity.

'It's Dad I'm mainly concerned about,' I said, with an exaggerated nod towards the house. 'Rich is really scared of Dad.'

'Yes, yes,' Mum agreed, a bit mollified. 'Your father's not good at talking to young people like I am.'

'And I hoped the article would get you to make Dad back off.'

'Yes… I see.'

We both stared at the soil again. A particularly large, disgusting worm was twisting across it.

'It was quite a good article, you know, India. Quite readable.'

'Thanks, Mum.'

'If you ever wanted to join Article Club, you know you'd be very welcome.'

'Thanks, I'll have a think about it … Mum?'

'Yes?'

'Do you want to do something together tomorrow? You can choose.'

'Really?' she said, her eyes shining.

'Yes,' I laughed.

'Great!'

We both turned and headed back inside.

'Andrew!' Mum called as she shut the door. 'Sorry, you can't do band practice tomorrow, I need you to go to the garden centre with me.'

'Oh.' Dad looked crestfallen and Mum winked at me.

I'd underestimated her. She did listen. She did understand me after all.

'It'll be after lunch though. In the morning, India and

I thought it'd be fun if we went on a speed walk in our active wear followed by a girls' coffee.'

No. No. NO.

She didn't understand ANYTHING at all.

Sunday morning. I woke Mum up with a cup of tea at seven-thirty. It was still dark outside. Excellent. I figured if I was going speed walking with her in matching outfits, I wanted to be doing it when as many people as possible were still asleep and, if they were awake, ideally when their vision was impaired.

'My, you're keen,' yawned Mum, sitting up in bed. 'Only trouble is, if we go now, only the park café will be open afterwards. I'd wanted to take you to my favourite one on the high street – Cup and Saucer.' I knew this would have been her plan. She loves Cup and Saucer. It's really popular with local mums who think it's edgy because it's modelled its style on somewhere in Hackney rather than deepest Surrey. The baristas have ironic moustaches and tattoos, you sit on upturned crates and there are floor to ceiling windows so everyone inside is highly visible to passers-by. There was no way I was sitting in there in hers-and-hers active wear.

'I love the park café,' I replied. '*Love* it.'

'Oh, right, OK then,' agreed Mum, slightly deflated.

Two pairs of strawberry leopard print legs with lace detail knees later we were ready to leave.

Or so I thought.

'Aren't you forgetting something?' Mum called as I opened the front door.

I stared back at her.

'Warm-up stretches!'

Dear God.

'I don't want to pull anything, India. Calf injuries are really painful.'

Twenty minutes of Mum stretching later we were ready to leave.

Or so I thought.

'I just need to find my water bottle, India. Have you seen my water bottle anywhere? You know the purple PLAHstic one.'

Does this woman ever leave the house?! Gritting my teeth, I stared at the hall clock. 8:30. Time was ticking by and the sun was now fully up. It was one of those bright winter days when everything is very, very clear.

'Maybe I left it in the car? Or in a bag after shopping?' she mused.

It was 8:45 when Mum finally called, 'Got it!' and we were off, weaving our way down the front path.

'Looking good, India,' came a squeaky call from somewhere. *What?!* My eyes darted around, horrified, only to land on the grinning form of Pete-the-child, leaning out of the window opposite.

'Isn't he a sweet boy,' Mum cooed as we took a left towards the park. 'He really seems to have taken a shine to you.' When he gets older and turns into a full-on stalker will she still think he's sweet then?

Luckily the streets were still pretty deserted. Sane people hadn't left the house yet. I walked faster than I've ever walked before. I was aiming to look like a blur.

'Wait for me, India!' Mum called and I slowed just enough for her to catch up, before ratcheting up the pace again. 'Netball practice really seems to have improved your fitness!' Mum panted beside me.

'Yup!' I gasped back, forcing my legs forward like pistons.

I glanced over at Mum to check she was keeping up. Her bum was wobbling from side to side. She looked ridiculous. Then I suddenly realised that mine was doing the same. That there was no way to actually speed walk and at the same time avoid the whole horrific butt-rocking motion.

We were through the entrance into the park and Mum seemed set on wobbling her way down the main path.

'Let's go the longer route,' I panted.

'OK,' Mum puffed back, surprised.

The longer route went round the edge of the park. The longer route hugged the trees and smelt slightly bad. No one chose the longer route.

We looped round the stagnant pond at the far end of the park and I then checked left and right. No one was coming. This was the perfect time to cut towards the centre where the café was.

Left right left right, wobble, wobble, wobble.

And done. We were standing outside the café and we still hadn't met anyone I knew.

Mum went inside and I waited on the decking area, eyes peeled, on high alert. She re-emerged a few minutes later with two polystyrene cups of Nescafé.

'Yum!' I said, cradling mine. The path was still empty. 'Right, let's head back.'

'We can't drink and walk!' Mum exclaimed. 'We'd burn ourselves. Here – let's perch on this log.'

I checked my watch. It was now past nine-thirty and the park was starting to fill up.

'Let's take off the plastic lids,' I suggested. 'It's terrible that they just automatically put them on. Think of the environment!'

Plastic lids are one of Mum's bugbears.

'Good idea, India. We'll be making a stand. PLAHstic lids, begone. We have no use for you!'

Plus the coffee will cool a lot quicker.

I dropped the lids into the bin as a few other people drifted in and out of the café. All old. Or families with young kids. I had just started to relax my guard a little when I saw them: a family of four, heading straight in my direction.

They came closer. There was something familiar about the way they walked. All of them. It was … unnecessarily bendy. They came closer still. It wasn't a family. It was two girls and two guys, about my age. At the front was a girl with ridiculously long thin legs and perfect, wafting blonde hair. Part of me died inside.

Lisa.

Don't draw attention to yourself. Don't draw attention to yourself.

'Isn't that someone from your class, India?' Mum said really loudly, pointing straight at Lisa. Lisa is a predator. Predators' attention is caught by movement.

'Be quiet, Mum,' I hissed, but it was too late.

Lisa sashayed closer and closer. Followed by April, Ennis and Anthony.

I could feel their eyes take me in. And then take Mum in.

Lisa and April started laughing. Dead-eyed, bow-lipped laughing. Openly. At us. Anthony looked confused. Ennis looked from me to my mum and back again, like a horrified metronome.

'Are they laughing at us?' Mum asked far too loudly. 'What rude girls! I've a good mind to have a go at them.'

'Mum, NOOOO!' I hissed.

'No one laughs at my daughter!'

'Mum, please can we just go?'

But Mum was having none of it. She'd turned tiger mum. Desperate to defend her cub's honour even though the cub just really wanted to go home.

'I know your type,' Mum said loudly, staring straight at Lisa, her right index finger jabbing the air. 'You think you're special just because you have long legs and blonde hair. Well, you're not. Go to Sweden and you'll find you're pretty average … because most Swedish girls have long legs and blonde hair.' *Yes, Mum, we got it.* Ennis's mouth was now hanging open.

'It's what's in here that counts.' Mum tapped the side of her head. 'Brains. Kindness.' *I'm not sure kindness is stored in your skull.* 'And India's got those in spades. And if she *chooses* to wear the same clothes as her mum,' I spat my mouthful of coffee everywhere, 'you should respect that.'

Then, with her head in the air, Mum pivoted and started speed walking off again. Left right left right. Wobble, wobble, wobble.

I jogged, numb, behind her, trying to ignore their chasing peals of laughter.

Mum, oblivious, had a smug smile on her lips.

'That girl…' she said.

'Lisa,' I supplied quietly. I couldn't feel my hands. I think I was in a state of shock.

'That *Lisa* should consider herself burnt. That's what you say, isn't it? *Burnt*. No one messes with the Smythe girls.'

School is going to be truly awful tomorrow.

It started before the first bell even rang.

'Is your Mum also in school uniform today?' April asked, mock-sweetly outside the Chemistry lab.

'Don't tease India,' purred Lisa. 'Her mum might come and tell us off.'

'Hahahahahahahaha.'

I sat at my allotted spot on the middle bench, next to Anna. She gave me a smile of support.

'Quieten down, Year 10!' shouted Mr Harold, unnecessarily loudly, sending his limp orange ponytail bobbing up and down. Maybe he's picked up some pointers from Ms Hatchard. Maybe he'll start using a whistle soon.

'Here are your test results.'

He stomped round the room, flinging down test papers in front of surprised-looking students. Something wasn't right. Where was the fake calmness? Where was the slightly too big patronising smile? I glanced around. Something was different about the room even. The whiteboard was the same. The test tubes were in the same place. The walls... Then I saw it, or rather didn't, the Learning Mountain poster. It was gone. Back in its original place was the periodic table. In monochrome.

My test landed in front of me with a thump.

52% was scrawled across the top in red biro. Oh dear. I normally did a lot better than that. Mum wasn't going to be thrilled.

'I am very disappointed in your tests. Very,' Mr Harold said, tiny bits of spittle fleeing from his mouth as he spoke.

'This is not difficult stuff. We covered it all in class. You just had to revise two topics. TWO! We're going to go through the paper together. Right, Question 1 ... How is an ionic bond formed ... anyone?'

Jenny Weir's hand shot up. Mr Harold ignored her.

'Anyone?'

Jenny Weir's hand reached even higher.

Everyone else's hand stayed resolutely down at bench height.

If he waited any longer Jenny Weir's arm was going to dislocate from its shoulder.

'Yes, Jenny,' said Mr Harold in a tired voice.

'By sharing electrons?'

'NO!' he exploded. 'That's what you wrote in the test. It is wrong. That's why there's a big red cross by it!'

'But isn't that good?' asked Jenny Weir, confused. 'Doesn't that mean I'm learning?'

'No, apparently it DOESN'T. Apparently none of you are learning ANYTHING! You're all going to sit in silence for the rest of the lesson while I dictate the CORRECT answers. For homework, you will then all write out the CORRECT answers again THREE TIMES.'

He was going old school. Properly old school. I never thought I'd miss our mountain leader.

I spent break hiding from Lisa and April in the library. Meena kept me company. I love the library. The mean kids never come here and the beanbags are really comfy. Mrs Greenwood, the librarian, saw that I looked a bit glum and snuck us both a custard cream even though we weren't helping re-stack the shelves. She's good like that. Meena made me replay the encounter between my mum and Lisa over and over. It started to get funny on the fourth retelling.

'I can't believe Ennis was there too,' she giggled.

'I know!'

'What did you ever see in him?'

'Um … I was never that keen, remember? It was you who thought I should go for Ennis.'

'I don't remember that.'

Meena has always had selective memory syndrome.

The rest of the day was filled with disappointing result after disappointing result. 49% in French. 53% in English. 51% in Geography. And so on. It seems that maybe I'm not that naturally bright after all. I think I'm actually one of those people who only do well if they study. Thank God these exams don't count!

I waited for Rich after school was over. I hadn't arranged to meet him or anything, I just really needed to see a friendly face. I didn't want to stand outside St Joseph's as I was bound to bump into Ennis and Anthony again and I felt too fragile to survive that. Instead, I worked out which road Rich normally turned up after saying goodbye to me and then I walked up that one and semi-hid behind someone's front hedge.

Typical classy girlfriend manoeuvre.

Just as I was beginning to think I'd missed him or was on the wrong road, I saw a wonderfully familiar high forehead approach.

'Hi!' I cried, jumping out from behind the hedge a little too enthusiastically.

Rich shot me a quick *am I dating a psycho-stalker* look before relaxing into a grin.

'India! … is everything OK?'

'Yes,' I said, smiling. Standing there, in front of him, everything did seem fine again. 'I just wanted to do this.' And I reached up and gave him a quick snog.

Tuesday.

A bad day.

A really, really bad day.

The morning was OK. We had Maths first thing and I'd actually done pretty well – 76% – because the good thing about Maths is, if you understand how to do it, there's not actually that much to revise. Then there was double Art and Mr Major is back! Back, I say! Goodbye Ms Roberts. And good riddance. I've never been so pleased to see a teacher's face before. I would have given him a hug if that wouldn't have involved us both being booked into appropriate teacher-student contact training. (Rumour has it that Mr Green had to go last week for chest-bumping Katie Forde in R.E.) We spent the lesson sketching a vase of flowers using charcoal and mine looked really life like and, best of all, Mr Major said that was a good thing.

So that morning (plus the bitter-sweet thrill of eating

my house's last packet of Monster Munch for lunch) did not prepare me in any way for the horrors of the afternoon.

Double Physics was straight after lunch.

Miss Haynes wasn't smiling as we entered the lab. But then she never normally is. She has the deathly pallor of someone who never goes outside. Or a corpse. And the personality to match.

She has a quiet, reedy voice and her eyes point in slightly different directions so it's not always that easy to tell who she's talking to.

She put our tests down in front of us weakly, as if the very action was spraining her wrist.

61%. Not so bad.

'Your papers confused me a little,' she warbled and then stared to the right, possibly out the window or possibly at Jasmine Wang. It was hard to tell. 'Some of you did very well indeed.' She nodded, this time definitely at Jasmine Wang, who looked annoyingly smug. I leant over to see her grade. 95%. OK, maybe justifiably smug.

'But the rest of you did pretty disappointingly in most questions … (a pause for about six seconds while she probably did a bit of daydreaming about the Hadron Collider) … but very well on the questions that concerned the order of the electromagnetic spectrum. I wonder why that was...' *Glance at the cupboard/possibly Tracy Williams.*

A cold shiver ran down my spine. Why did Meena have to have told so many people about my mnemonic thing? No one would mention it now, would they? Surely not?

'It's because of the memory thing,' piped up the genius that is Jenny Weir.

What? Shut up! Shut up!

Thirty necks swivelled in her direction.

'What do you mean?' quavered Miss Haynes.

'You know ... the Rachel's Mum thing.'

'*I* don't know,' growled Rachel, leaning forward on her stool. Her arms looked strong in that position. Wiry. I'd never noticed how strong and wiry Rachel's arms were.

'You know, *Rachel's Mum Is*,' continued Jenny Weir, completely unphased. She really has zero social barometer.

'It seems like some of us don't,' replied Miss Haynes, 'but I do like memory techniques. Perhaps you should come up and write it on the board.'

No. No. NO.

What were my options? I couldn't run and rugby tackle Jenny Weir to the floor, could I? I turned to Meena for advice. She just gave my hand a little squeeze like a priest who's attending a criminal sentenced to hang.

Jenny Weir was now at the front, pen raised to the

whiteboard. I looked on horror-struck as she wrote out the words.

Rachel's Mum Is Very Ugly X Gillian

Miss Haynes seemed to be frozen to the spot.

The air was static.

My pulse reverberated in my ears. Boom. Boom. Boom.

Then, with a blood-curdling roar, Rachel Turner leapt out of her seat, stomach surfed over the bench in front and started pummelling Gillian. She'd misinterpreted the 'Gillian'. She'd seen it as a sort of signature.

'How could you?!' she was shouting.

Gillian was defending herself (and looking like she was actually enjoying it a bit).

'Gillian! I'm very surprised by this,' quavered Miss Haynes, not even attempting to break up the fight.

I took a deep breath. I knew what I had to do. And I knew how it would go down.

'Rachel,' I said, far too quietly. Rachel kept thumping Gillian. 'Rachel,' I repeated, a bit louder, 'I'm really sorry, it wasn't Gillian who invented that… It was me.'

Rachel looked up from Gillian and started to stalk towards me. Gillian grabbed her from behind and held her back.

'It wasn't about you. Or your mum – who's very pretty, by the way,' (best pretend I hadn't seen the other one). 'I'm so, so sorry. I was trying to work out a way of

124

remembering the electromagnetic spectrum and the words just sort of popped into my head. I didn't know everyone would start using it.' *Quick glare at Meena.*

I think Rachel saw that I was genuinely sorry as she stopped pulling away from Gillian and sat back down on her stool.

'Rachel, India and Gillian,' declared Miss Haynes. 'See me after class.'

When the end of lesson bell rang, everyone else filed out the room and the three of us shuffled to the front.

I got detention for my 'ill-advised revision methods'. Rachel had to apologise to Gillian for hitting her and got detention too.

'Violence is n… n…ever the answer,' Miss Haynes stammered, 'even if there's been ex… ex…treme provocation.'

I apologised to Rachel again as we left the classroom and headed towards the hall.

'It's OK,' she said. 'I overreacted a bit. It's just that people can be idiots about my mums so I get quite protective. Most people aren't. But some are.'

'Sorry to hear that,' I said sincerely. 'I didn't know. I thought everyone our age was above that sort of rubbish.' I couldn't believe it. How can you get to fourteen or fifteen and care if someone has two mums or two dads? Seriously?

'And one of my mums can be quite shouty at matches which doesn't help.'

'Really?' I said, feigning ignorance.

She looked sad so I wracked my brain for something to cheer her up.

'My Dad's decided to join my boyfriend's band.'

'Has he? Has he really?' Rachel grinned. 'Ha ha. That's worse. That's definitely worse.'

Wednesday morning.

'An average of 54% and a detention!' Mum exploded as I crunched on my first mouthful of 5% sugar Cheerios.

Good morning to you too, Mum.

'I just got an email about it from your form teacher. It must be serious if I'm getting an email at 7:12am!'

'Everyone did badly,' I mumbled.

'No. Not everyone got a detention. Not everyone's parents got an email from their daughter's form teacher at 7:12am!'

I couldn't help but feel that undue significance was being placed on the time stamp. Maybe Mrs Johnson was like one of those absurd actors – going to bed ridiculously early and then waking up at five to have an ice shower before going to the gym to work on their exaggerated biceps and eight pack? I pictured Mrs Johnson bench pressing pre-dawn whilst sipping a wheat grass shot. No, I don't think so.

'That's it, India,' cried Mum, interrupting my rather disturbing daydream, 'I'm getting you a tutor!'

'I don't want a tutor!' I blurted out. No, that wasn't the right way to deal with this new threat. I had to be calm. Rational. Appeal to our new mother-daughter bond. '...I don't need a tutor. I just need to revise a bit more. Us *Smythe girls* can do it by ourselves.'

'You're having a tutor.'

Damn. Didn't work.

'But Mum—'

'Don't be so ungrateful. Do you know how expensive tutors are?'

'I don't want one!'

'Sometimes, India... *Huuuufffff.'*

She was gone.

And I seem to be getting at tutor.

'Maybe you'll get a hot tutor?' Meena suggested at break. 'He'll be all, "And the imagery in this bit of the poem is very significant because of blah blah blah," and you'll be all, "Melt me with your smoking eyes."'

We collapsed laughing while Anna looked on confused.

'Actually a tutor could be really beneficial to you,' Anna said seriously. 'He could open your eyes to the deeper meaning of the set texts.'

'With his smoking hot eyes … hahahahaha,' added Meena.

'No,' I replied, ignoring Meena. 'I just didn't revise properly. And why would the tutor be a guy anyway?'

'Are you worried that you'll fall for him and forget about Rich?' Meena asked seriously.

'No. Don't be ridiculous.'

'Exactly how into Rich are you?'

'I'm into him. I'm really into him.'

'Do you love him?'

Love.

That word.

Hmmmm. I really like Rich. I miss him when he's not there and think about him all the time. Is that love? Do I even want to love him if he's so certain that he doesn't love me?

'There's only one way to find out for sure,' Meena declared.

'What's that?'

'Take a love survey.'

'Really?'

'Definitely.'

'What's the scientific basis of the love survey?' Anna asked, genuinely interested.

Meena shot her a look of disgust.

'You wouldn't understand. Science doesn't explain everything. Although this does have a bit of astronomy in, I think.'

'Do you mean astrology?' asked Anna.

'Same thing.'

I'm beginning to think I should donate the tutor to Meena.

Meena took out her phone and did a quick Google search.

'OK, this one's got four stars which means it's really reliable.'

I nodded my head. I was ready. *Survey, tell me – am I in love with Rich Evans?*

'OK,' Meena began. 'It's really important that you give your honest answer. Don't overthink it. Go with your gut. Are you ready?'

'Yes.'

'Question 1: if you could spend a weekend with him would you prefer to go to:

(a) Paris

(b) a secluded mountain hut

(c) a water park?'

Right. Hmmm. I'd like to do all three. I think Paris is probably the in-love answer. Or maybe it's the mountain hut. Just us, some sheepskins and rocks. Sounds a bit boring. Don't overthink, brain. I really like water parks. I think Rich would like them too. I think we'd have lots of fun at a water park.

'c.' Meena's eyebrows shot up.

'Question 2: when you think about him do you think about:

(a) his eyes

(b) his body

(c) his smile?'

I waited to see if there was a '(d) his forehead', but there wasn't. It was a choice of 'a' and 'c'. I know eyes are supposedly windows to your soul, but it was his smile I probably thought about most. His smile and his dimples.

'c'. Meena smiled knowingly. She was starting to annoy me.

'Third and final question.' *Really? Just 3? Whether or not I was in love was going to be determined this quickly?* 'If he was an animal do you think he'd be:

(a) a lion

(b) a horse

(c) a chipmunk?'

I hesitated. I wanted Rich to be a lion. Strong and majestic. But then I closed my eyes and imagined him waving his hair around like a mane and I cracked up.

'Remember, don't overthink it,' instructed Meena seriously. 'Go with your gut.'

Horse? No, not really. Gallopy gallop. Shut up, brain. There was only one possible answer.

'c,' I said. Rich was most like a chipmunk. But that wasn't a bad thing. I like chipmunks. They're sweet and friendly.

Meena's face was troubled.

'So?' I asked.

She took a deep breath.

'Three 'c's,' she said sombrely. 'I'm sorry, but it's not going to work out between you two.'

Wait a minute? I thought we were seeing if I was in love, not if we were going to work out?

'All 'c's means you're destined to just be friends. You're not in love with Rich Evans and it's very unlikely that he's in love with you.'

I sat there in silence.

'Think about it, India,' Meena said more gently. 'A water park? A *chipmunk*?!?'

I thought about it. Hearing my answers repeated back, they didn't sound too good. There aren't exactly many films about a couple desperately in love zooming down a water slide. And a chipmunk? A chipmunk might be the least sexy animal of all time.

Back home after school I was getting a snack from the kitchen (an individually wrapped portion of malt loaf – pretty rubbish compared to normal snacks but a result for the Smythe household), when my phone beeped.

It was a text from Rich, seeing if I could go round to his after school tomorrow. I felt a bit nervous reading it. I've never been to his before. I'd spent so much time worrying about him meeting my parents and then dealing with the fallout from that that I'd kind of forgotten that the other way round might have to happen too. At least there was just one parent to meet – Rich's parents split up a while ago and he just lives with his mum. When I started getting over the fear, part of me began to feel a little bit pleased. Rich clearly *wanted* me to meet his mum. He wanted to show me off. That's not the behaviour of someone who's 'just a friend'. That's proper boyfriend behaviour. The sort of behaviour of someone in a couple on the path to love.

I checked with Mum if it'd be OK. She doesn't

normally let me go out mid-week, but I thought she'd make an exception for Rich.

'No, tomorrow won't work, I'm afraid.'

'But—'

'There's no point arguing, India. I've booked a tutor for tomorrow. He's coming from 6:30 to 7:30. And you've got netball practice before then and your homework after that.'

'I can skip netball. Can't we rearrange the lesson?'

'His name is Oliver,' Mum continued, completely ignoring me. 'He taught Michelle down the road's son. Michelle said he was really good.' Mum's tone lowered slightly. '…And a bit of a hunk… Here, see for yourself.' Mum winked at me then whipped out her phone and googled something.

I felt slightly sick. The 'Smythe girls' never discussed the hotness of guys. The 'Smythe girls' never exchanged winks over the hotness of guys. And now was not the time to start. It was highly inappropriate. I had a serious boyfriend who, contrary-to-online-survey-which-knew-absolutely-nothing, was definitely not just my friend. And Mum … well, Mum had Dad.

Mum thrust the phone in my face. There, under the serious-looking navy banner of Robson Tutors (for all your tuition needs) the face of Oliver Chambers stared back at me. He was not hot. There was nothing that wrong with his features themselves but he was radiating smugness. You could tell he was the sort of guy who probably wore chinos and a white shirt. Awful.

I tried again.

'Can't we just move the lesson?'

'No, India, we can't. You have to pay in advance and it's very expensive.'

I rolled my eyes. I didn't ask them to waste their money. Sighing, I texted Rich back.

'Can't do tomorrow, I'm afraid. How about Fri? xx'

'OK. Cool. Mum will be in then though. Shall we go out? xx'

Oh. He hadn't wanted me to meet his mum after all. I felt very insulted. He'd met my parents. Why didn't he want me to meet his mum? Was he embarrassed of me? Did he think this wasn't a proper thing? That he wasn't at the 'introduce girlfriend to mum' stage?

'No. It's fine. I'll come round. xx'

Try and wriggle out of that one.

'If you're sure J'

Hmmm. Now even the kisses were gone. All I was getting was a smiley face. That did seem to be a pretty annoyingly clear sign of just friendship.

'Sure.' I pressed send.

No kisses *or* smiley face. Read into that what you will, Rich Evans.

Thursday.

I decided that having Netball Club and a tutor on the same day would probably destroy me so at registration I asked Gillian if she'd tell Ms Hatchard that I wasn't coming any more. Simple, pretty reasonable request, you might think. Apparently not. Gillian stepped away from me, mouth open in shock.

'That's not how it's done, India!' she exclaimed. 'That's completely against the Sporting Code of Honour!'

'There's a Sporting Code of Honour?'

'Of course! I can't believe you don't know that! And rule number one is: you don't desert your team.' *Spoken like I was going to abandon my fellow soldiers on the front line and drive off in the only tank.* 'And if you are … a … a deserter,' she nearly choked on the word, 'at least have the balls to tell the squadron leader yourself!!'

'Netball Club has a squadron leader?'

'Ms Hatchard. Obviously.'

Right.

I spotted Ms Hatchard on the games field at first break and thought I'd get it over and done with. I approached and hovered a little distance away, trying to gauge her mood.

'India, what are you hovering there for?' Ms Hatchard barked.

I'd say her mood was slightly irritated. With me.

'Um… Ms Hatchard, I just wanted to let you know … Sporting Code of Honour and all that…'

Ms Hatchard looked thoroughly confused. I'm not sure Gillian's right about the whole code thing existing. '…That I'm not going to be able to make Netball Club any more.'

'And why's that?' asked Ms Hatchard, her eyes narrowing to slits, secret police interrogator style.

'It's just I've got a tutor coming on Thursdays now.'

'How nice for you.' Her tone was ice. 'And what time is this *tutor* coming?'

'6:30.'

What? Why did I say that? It's the truth but I meant to lie. I meant to say five.

'Netball Club is over by 5:30 so it won't be a problem.'

'But I might be too tired.'

'Are you *tired* after Netball Club?' she spat with maximum possible disdain.

'Um … yes.'

Truly. Utterly. Exhausted.

'Well, that means you're unfit.

'Err…'

'Do you *want* to be unfit?'

'Err...'

'Well? It's a simple question. Do you, India Smythe, want to be unfit and die young?'

I couldn't say 'yes'. *Yes, I quite like being unfit. I quite like sitting around, pretending to go on a bike ride while eating Monster Munch even if that might, over time, slightly impact on my longevity.* I had to say 'no'. 'No' was the only acceptable answer.

'Err ... no.'

'Then I'll see you after school.'

'Right.'

Damn.

Seems like I'll be a member of Netball Club for the rest of my life.

As predicted, I was exhausted when the tutor arrived at 6:28pm with a smug look-how-great-I-am-because-I'm-here-two-minutes-early smile.

'Hi, I'm Oliver.' He pronounced it Ol-i-ver, drawing out each syllable as if it was a really exciting, unusual name. 'Lovely to meet you, Mrs Smythe... And you must be India.'

Wow. Sherlock Holmes himself. He spoke to me like he was generations above me even though he couldn't have been a day over twenty-two. Mum gave me a wink over his shoulder. Another, *here's your hot tutor – you're welcome* sick-inducing wink. In the flesh, Oliver was still not hot. Not hot at all. He thought he was, clearly. You could tell by the unnecessary scarf that wafted round his neck and just happened to accentuate his blue eyes. *And* the fact that he had longish, floppy brown hair that he managed to peer fake-sheepishly out of like a chef on the cover of a recipe book. *Here's little old me peeping out of a bunch of chard.* BTW he *was* wearing chinos and a white shirt. It's like I'm too good at this. I wonder what jobs involve predicting exactly what's going to happen. Maybe I could be one of those *Minority Report* Precogs but sit on a sofa telling people stuff rather than having to lie submerged in a weird bath?

'Let's begin!' he cried, rubbing his hands together. 'Where are we working?'

'In the kitchen, if you don't mind me getting on with dinner?' Mum suggested, practically drooling out the side of her mouth. No way. There was no way I was going to do a one-on-one lesson with Mum hovering around in the background on heat.

'In my room,' I said flatly. 'We'll do it at the desk in my room.'

'Right ho!' said Oliver. *No one under fifty should ever say 'right ho'.* 'Lead the way.'

Sighing inside, I took him upstairs. He sat at my desk and I went to get another chair. On my return I shut the door behind me.

'Oh no!' he cried, leaping to his feet and rushing to the door. 'The door must remain slightly open at all times. You know. So we both *feel safe*.'

He left the door open about two feet.

Was he insinuating what I thought he was insinuating? I sat on the chair next to him and my knee accidentally knocked into his. He flinched away as if I was radioactive and then made a massive show about putting his legs as far away from mine as possible.

He shot me another patronising smile. 'Let's try and concentrate, shall we?' Oh. My. God. He was. He was insinuating exactly what I thought he'd been insinuating. He thought *I* thought he was hot. He thought *I* was trying to hit on him. The horror. The shame.

'What subject shall we start with? Your mother said you were struggling with everything.'

Thanks, Mum.

'No, I just didn't revise for my tests.'

'Yes, I see.' He didn't believe me at all.

'Let's start with Chemistry.'

'No. I'm actually normally quite good at Chemistry.'

'Well… How about English then? Some creative exercises? There's a really fun one I do with my students where I shout out the name of a colour, a piece of fruit and an animal and they have to weave them together into a one sentence story.'

I don't think that's on the GCSE curriculum.

'We could go through the set poems?' I suggested. 'I never really got *My Last Duchess.*'

'Oh, OK,' he said. 'Let me read it first.'

After a few minutes of silence while he read through the poem, brow furrowed, he came up with lots of super-obvious comments. This was pointless. Completely pointless. I felt it almost impossible to even pretend to concentrate. Finally the hour was up.

'How did it go?' Mum asked brightly from the kitchen as I trudged down the stairs.

I said nothing.

'Good … good,' Oliver said. 'India found it slightly hard to concentrate at first – (*unnecessary flick of floppy hair*) – it's quite normal at her age' (*I'm maximum eight years younger than you!!*) 'But then I managed to get her involved a bit more.' (*No you didn't.*)

'OK. Well, thank you so much for everything, Oliver, and we'll see you next week.'

'Yes, see you then, Mrs S.' (*Deliberate lowering of fringe and full-on chef chard smile.*)

Mum followed him to the door, cheeks flushed, grinning all the way.

'Well, Oliver's *very* nice,' she said as soon as it was just us again in the hall.

'Hmmmph,' I replied. I wanted to say more, but I didn't want to upset her. I knew the lessons were expensive.

'And try to concentrate more. I know it's distracting for you being around such a hunk, but try. These lessons are very expensive.'

'So … how was the tutor?' Meena asked as soon as she saw me come through the school gates. 'Did he melt you with his smoking eyes?'

We both cracked up.

'He wasn't hot at all.'

'I bet he was. Just a little.'

'Who was?' Anna had now joined us.

'India's tutor,' Meena explained. 'Most super-clever guys are pretty hot. There's just something about them I find … alluring.' Spoken as if she'd had millions of super-clever boyfriends.

'Well, Ol-i-ver doesn't seem super-clever. And he's

definitely not hot. Look, I'll prove it to you,' I said. 'Give me your phone.'

Meena handed it over and I googled Robson Tutors and found Oliver Chambers' face. It didn't take long. The agency only had about three tutors. Their claim to be 'Surrey's leading tutor provider' was beginning to look a bit shaky.

'Oh, no!' Meena exclaimed.

'Oh … hot!' said Anna.

It didn't surprise me that Anna had mum-taste in guys.

'He wears chinos and a white shirt too,' I added.

'Oh, *no*!' repeated Meena.

'Nice!' said Anna.

But it wasn't Oliver I wanted to talk to them about. It was Rich. I explained the whole me-inviting-myself-round-to-meet-his-mum thing.

'What do you think it means?' I asked.

Meena shot me a really sympathetic yet patronising look.

'Simple. He doesn't see your relationship going anywhere. Why introduce a girl to your mum if you're then going to have to explain in a couple of weeks why she isn't around any more?'

Wow.

Knife in the chest.

Not only was my relationship not really going anywhere, I was also about to be dumped.

'Thanks, Meena, thanks a lot.'

I stormed off down the corridor.

Ms Hatchard stopped me as I rounded the corner. I thought she was going to have a go at me. School's got some ridiculous no-one-can-walk-over-3-mph policy in case of a fatal collision. But she didn't. She asked if I was all right. And she looked concerned.

'It's important that us athletes stick together,' she said.

Athletes. No one had ever called me an athlete before. I liked it.

'Thanks,' I replied.

'No problem. It's rule two of the Sporting Code of Honour.'

Oh my God.

It does exist.

It was Friday night and rather than being out somewhere having fun with Rich I was standing on the pavement outside his house, plucking up the courage to ring the bell and meet his mum.

What the hell had I been thinking?

By forcing Rich into this meetup was I pushing too hard? Was he going to end up dumping me this evening rather than in a fortnight's time?

I checked my watch again. Five past had turned into ten past. If I didn't enter soon I'd end up being properly late and make a terrible first impression.

I did three rescue breaths. Mum showed them to me recently. She did them at yoga. You basically do three massive breaths in quick succession and send loads of oxygen all round the body to make you feel calm but alert at the same time.

Hoooooop. Hoooooop. Hoooooop.

I now felt slightly dizzy and rather sick.

It'll be OK, I told myself. The cottage was lovely. It was tiny, the window frames were painted pale blue and there was a yellow rose climbing up the walls and a pot of plants by the front door. Surely only someone nice and friendly could live here?

I forced my legs forward and finger upwards.

Briiiiinngggg.

Rich opened the door immediately, a big grin on his face.

'Come in,' he said, pulling me inside. 'My mum's still out so we've got a bit of time together.'

Still holding my hand, he gave me the tour.

Downstairs was the living room with kitchen at one end. Upstairs was a bathroom, his mum's room and …

'…this is my room.'

I followed him inside, my heart beating faster. I'd never been in a boy's room before. Not a boy who was a boyfriend. My boyfriend. I was in my boyfriend's room!

I looked around, taking it all in. Looking for insights into the mind of Rich Evans. Hmmm. He was either weirdly neat or had made a massive effort to tidy before I came round as the bed and desk were clear and no clothes were spilling out of his chest of drawers. There was a desk in the corner and a bookcase. The walls were light blue and covered with loads of posters of bands I'd never heard of. The only one I knew was *Vampire Weekend*. I have their *Father of the Bride* album. It's pretty good.

I said so and he put it on.

Rich sat down on his bed. The duvet cover was light blue too. I sat down next to him, upright and awkward.

How long was his mum going to be out for? I'd basically invited myself round… I hope he didn't think…

Then Rich seemed to sense what I was thinking and got all flustered and was all, 'I hope you don't think … oh … um…'

So we just sat next to each other in silence for a bit, pretending to listen to the music. *Suuun flow-er in the mor-ning...* Finally he put his right arm round my shoulders and I leant my head against his chest. It was nice. More than nice.

He leant in and I leant in and next thing we were kissing. Really kissing. It couldn't be just friendship. I really like Meena but I don't want to kiss her like this.

Then he was kissing my neck, and his hand, the one that had just been resting on the duvet, started to move upwards. It was still on the outside of my T-shirt but it was definitely rising northwards. Chestwards. It was like the realisation fractured my brain in two. Part of it was pleased. But the other part of it was thinking *oh no he's going to finally realise how very small my boobs are*. His hand was level with my belly button when there was a sudden noise from the landing.

'Hello!!!!!!'

What?

Aggggghhhhhhhh.

There, framed in the light of the doorway, was Rich's mum.

How had we not heard her come in? The music wasn't that loud. Was she some sort of stealth ninja?

Worst of all, Rich seemed to be suffering some sort of shock paralysis and was frozen to the spot, hand still in position, edging towards my right boob. I pushed it away and leapt to my feet.

146

I thought about what would happen if Mum found me in my room with a boy. She'd go ballistic. I'd be grounded till I was thirty. I forced myself to look at Rich's mum. To meet her gaze. I couldn't believe what I saw. She was … smiling. Beaming, in fact.

'You must be India, I've heard all about you.'

She can't have seen the hand. She can't have seen us snogging. Waves of relief crashed over me.

'Good evening, Mrs…' and then I paused. She wasn't Mrs Evans any more. They'd got divorced. I had no idea what she was now.

'I'm Lou,' she said, smiling again. She had dimples too. Not quite as deep as Rich's, but in the exact same place.

Then her expression changed and became super-serious then weirdly excited.

'Oh, yes … that might work. I'll be back in a second.'

With that she was gone and I heard a rustling from the other room. *Thanks, hearing, for returning again. Where were you when I needed you?*

I sat back down on the bed.

'What's going on?' I whispered to Rich.

'I've no idea,' Rich mumbled back. 'She just gets random ideas sometimes.'

A second later she was back in the doorway. Holding a camera.

A big, professional-looking camera.

What the hell?!? I sprang off the bed.

'Sorry to startle you,' she said. 'It's just that I've got an exhibition coming up. It's called *Intense* and it's really all about capturing the human experience. I've been missing the final image and when I saw you two together just now I knew I'd found it. Would you let me photograph you?'

My first thought was – ha! Love Survey, take that! We give off such intense vibes that his mum wants to put us in her show!! My second thought was a photo of us snogging? In his bedroom?? Absolutely no way. Never. She read my horrified face.

'No, not here!' she laughed. 'Gosh no. Downstairs on the sofa. No touching. Just sitting side by side, not even looking at each other. Your subconscious body language will tell the story.'

'Muummmm, no,' hissed Rich.

'Maybe it'd be OK?' I said. I'd never had my picture taken by a professional photographer before. And, it'd be nice to have one of us together, radiating our intense emotions.

'You don't have to do this, India,' he said.

'No, I want to,' I replied firmly.

We followed his mum downstairs and she told us, 'Just sit down, side by side, however feels right. Don't look at each other, just *feel* the proximity.'

Rich sat awkwardly. I sat next to him. I tried to relax my body but it was all tense. I could feel a muscle in my cheek. I'd never felt a muscle in my cheek before. Hopefully it wouldn't show. Like a weird mid-face bicep.

Click. Click.

Quick pause as his mum adjusted the lighting.

Click.

'Perfect. It couldn't be more perfect. The exhibition's next month. You'll come, won't you, India?'

'Sure,' I smiled.

'And feel free to bring some friends.'

I can't wait to see Meena's face.

'Right … look at the time! Would you two love birds like some dinner?' she continued, 'I can make a mean carbonara.'

'Yes please,' I said. I was properly hungry and love all forms of pasta.

'Wonderful. I'll get cracking. You can either stay down here or go upstairs and explore each other's bodies for another fifteen minutes?'

My mouth fell open as I double-checked her face. No. She wasn't being sarcastic. She *had* seen us snogging. She *had* seen his hand inching upwards. And now she was giving us the genuine option to continue. Oh my God.

'We'll stay down here,' Rich spluttered.

At least mine aren't the only embarrassing parents in the world.

Back at school, I told the gang all about Rich's mum walking in on us.

Meena found it hilariously funny.

'And his mum definitely saw you snogging?'

I nodded, prompting an explosive, 'Hahahahahahahahhaha.'

'And she definitely said, 'Explore each other's bodies?'

I nodded again.

'Hahahahahahahaha.'

'And was it definitely your right boob?' asked Anna.

We all turned to look at her.

'Why is that important?'

'I don't know,' said Anna quietly, clearly out of her depth. 'I just wanted to join in.'

Then I told them about the photography exhibition and asked if they'd like to come.

Their reaction wasn't quite what I was hoping for.

Meena: Don't keep going on about it.

I've just mentioned it. That was the mention.

Gillian: Maybe. If I'm not playing or watching sport.

That'll be a 'no' then.

Anna: I love exhibitions. I'm always going to them at the Science Museum. Do you think they'll let us look inside the cameras to see how they work?

Not quite the point.

I can't believe they weren't being more supportive. When it's all *let's laugh at India's incredibly embarrassing life* they're all over it. When it's *let's go and see India looking intense and in love in a very important photography exhibition by a probably very famous and important photographer* they lose interest.

Anna and Gillian I could forgive as they never got stuff like this, but Meena, it was exactly the sort of thing she normally liked.

I made another attempt at drawing her in.

'When his mum saw us together, snogging, she was so taken aback by how in love we were that she said she *had* to take the photo. She said it was the final piece. That we completed her exhibition. Her exhibition is called *Intense*.'

Still nothing. I think she might be jealous. Of how in love we are.

Finally Meena deigned to speak.

'We'll come to your exhibition.' *How good of you.* 'But remember, the survey doesn't lie. You're sounding a bit desperate to prove that you're in love with him. But we all heard it, India. *Water Park... Chipmunk.*'

And with that, she walked away, trying to look all wise professor from high-end university.

She kept up her annoyingness for the whole day so it was therefore quite nice to get home to some good news.

Dad bounced in the door after work, the first words off his lips, 'We're going away at half term!'

We never go away at half term. We never go away at Easter. We are purely summer-holiday goer away-ers.

'Where?' I asked excitedly.

'Greece! Corfu. Kev's getting married and I'm going to be best man. It's just for a few days.'

Kev. Dad's old bandmate. Getting married. Dad looked inexplicably happy at the prospect.

'Why do you look so happy?' Mum asked, suspicious. 'You don't normally like going away and you hate weddings.' She was also probably gearing up to get into a bad mood as she thinks Kev is a bad influence and that Dad shouldn't spend time with him. Also they've got history. I don't think she knows that Dad told me that she used to date Kev and Dad sort of stole her off him.

'No reason. No reason,' Dad said, trying to look casual and failing. 'It's just Kev's been single for so long…'

That's true. Kev never got married. Never gave up music to become a dentist. The rare times we saw him he always had a different girlfriend with him. Always some new leggy blonde in her early twenties.

'…Do him good to get tied down,' Dad continued, the smirk as impossible to remove from his face as if he'd drawn it on in Sharpie, '…see how the rest of us live. See that it's not all fun and late nights and gigs and … fun.'

'Is that so?' said Mum, tight-lipped as she left the room. I think she felt the second 'fun' was a bit unnecessary.

Still, Mum would soon come round and the fact remained – we were going to Greece at half term!!!

Thursday came round again. Netball Club had been cancelled because Ms Hatchard was ill – hooray! (*hope it's nothing serious or I'll feel really guilty*) – and I was busy doing English upstairs in my room. My rubbish test results scared me a bit and my notes from class are beyond useless. Our English teacher, Mrs Parker, had this stupid idea that we should all teach each other different aspects of the set texts as that way we 'come together as a group' and 'achieve a sense of ownership' of the work. It's ridiculous. It doesn't work at all. Aren't teachers supposed to know a bit more about a subject than the students? Aren't they supposed to be imparting some of this superior knowledge?

We're doing *Macbeth* this term and so far we've had a presentation by Lisa and April on the symbolism of blood on hands and my notes now consist of some bullet points saying that maybe blood is as hard to remove as nail varnish. That maybe they didn't have the equivalent of nail varnish remover at that time and that's why Lady Macbeth had to keep washing her hands to try to remove that 'damned spot'. Seriously. I can just picture examiners' mouths dropping open in horror. Tomorrow Jenny Weir and Natasha Corn are going to be telling us about the significance of sleep in the play. I don't have high hopes.

Anyway, I was busy looking at a combination of SparkNotes and the actual play when Mum yelled from downstairs.

'Oliver's here.'

Damn. I'd forgotten.

He was at the top of the stairs by the time I opened my bedroom door. He came inside with a 'please try to resist me' smile and made a show of leaving the door wide open behind him.

'Right, so what shall we cover today? Maybe some History?'

'Sure,' I said. 'Some help in History might be good.'

'OK. Let's start with the Vietnam War.'

'I'm not doing the Vietnam War.'

'Oh. Arthur down the road is doing the Vietnam War,' he said accusatorially.

'We're doing the Russian Revolution.'

'Oh. I don't know much about that. I could read your textbook?'

That wasn't very reassuring.

'Do you *teach* History?' I asked.

'Of course,' he snapped back.

'How about the Versailles Treaty?' I suggested.

Nope. He didn't know that either. I listed topic after

topic. Doubt was spreading over his face. His hair seemed limper. His eyes less shiny.

'The Weimar Republic?'

'Yes,' he said, a drowning man scrambling into a life raft. 'I know about that one. Let's make a mind map.'

He started droning on about the Weimar Republic and made me put all these points onto a giant mind map. But I couldn't concentrate. I'd stupidly put a wool jumper over my T-shirt and it wasn't even that cold as Mum had the heating on for once. I was getting hotter and hotter. Beads of sweat were starting to form on my forehead. I needed to take the jumper off.

'Sorry, just a minute,' I said. 'It's a bit hot in here.'

I leant back, making sure I didn't accidentally touch Oliver in the process and started to peel off the jumper. It was halfway over my head when I heard his strangled gasp.

'No! Stop! No!'

What the hell? Then I felt it. Cold air against skin. Cold air against my stomach skin. Oh my God. My T-shirt must had risen up with my jumper the way they sometimes do. I had just flashed my tutor.

And … and he thought I'd done it on purpose.

I quickly pulled the jumper back down over my head, my face flaming red.

'I'm so sorry about that,' I mumbled. But Oliver

wasn't looking at me. He'd taken a small black notebook out of his backpack. He flicked to something written on the second or third page in.

I could just read the heading. Incident Report Procedure.

He scanned the page, then flicked to the next empty page and began to write. He spoke aloud as he formed the words.

'The time is 6:43pm. I was with the student, India Smythe, when she said that "it is hot in here".' He paused momentarily and looked at me, pen raised.

'Did you say "hot in here" or "steamy" or "hot and steamy"?'

'Hot,' I whispered. I didn't say 'steamy'. I've never said 'steamy'.

Pen made contact with paper again.

'She said that it was *hot* in here. The student then intentionally bared her stomach at me in a provocative manner. I did not respond. I moved away.'

I was no longer breathing. My body had forgotten how to inhale.

Oliver flicked back to the Procedure page. There it was. Finger on bullet point four. Inform parent immediately.

Oliver picked up his backpack and coat and left the room. I sat there. Eyes fixed on my desk, setting the world record for longest time a person has spent without oxygen.

I heard low voices from the hall and the noise of the front door shutting.

Mum appeared at the door to my room moments later. She was going to go mad.

But she didn't. It was worse than that. She 'tried to understand'.

'I didn't intentionally flash him, Mum. I was taking my jumper off. Because it was too hot. And my T-shirt got caught.'

'Teenage years are a difficult time,' Mum said, as if having a completely different conversation with a completely different person. 'All those feelings. Those urges.'

'It was a mistake, Mum. A mistake.'

'Obviously, Oliver feels that he shouldn't come back. That if he comes back it might only encourage your feelings for him.'

'I don't have any feelings for him!'

'And young men have to be so careful nowadays what situations they put themselves in.'

'I was taking off a jumper. It was a hot-room situation.'

'We won't tell your father.'

At least we could agree on one thing.

'And we might leave the tutoring for a while.'

Thank God.

'In case we get another attractive one.'

Aggggghhhhhh.

'Are you *sure* it was an accident?' Meena asked seriously as our class walked down the freezing outside path towards assembly. 'It's definitely not just that you know things aren't going that well with Rich so you wanted to flash your stomach at Ol-i-ver just to get some male attention?'

'No!' I shouted indignantly.

'Quiet, India,' yelled Mrs Johnson.

'It might be your subconscious acting?' Meena whispered. 'I don't think my top has ever lifted up with my jumper. I don't think that's a thing.'

'Of course it's a thing. Anna, Gillian, back me up.'

'I don't know…' said Anna doubtfully.

'I don't care,' said Gillian.

We sat next to each other in the hall. Even the hall was freezing. There was one tiny plug-in heater at the front to heat whatever teacher was on stage. The rest of us were left to turn into blocks of ice. The words of a hymn were projected onto the screen at the front. Damn, I'd forgotten it was hymn practice. Mrs Trent stalked to the front of the hall. Not good. It was going to be far harder to maintain this very important conversation when Daredevil-level hearing was in charge. I still got the occasional flashback to the time she made me sing a solo of *All Things Bright and Beautiful* in front of the whole school. Just for talking.

'Look!' hissed Meena. She was tugging up her jumper while pointing at her shirt. 'It's still in place.'

I didn't want to speak. I really didn't. But I couldn't let that stand.

'That's because it's tucked in,' I whispered. 'My top wasn't tucked in.' Honestly, why can't they get it? Surely this isn't a phenomenon that only I've come across? I can't have some weird genetic skin condition that repels T-shirts, can I?

'Is someone talking?' yelled Mrs Trent from the front. I stared intensely at the floor. Maybe she was like a T-Rex. Maybe she only noticed movement.

I felt her eyes laser past me. Past me. I was safe.

Meena poked me in the ribcage and mouthed Ol-i-ver while forming a heart shape with her hands.

That was it. I had to prove to her how wrong she was. I poked her back and untucked my shirt then in one swift movement I hoisted my jumper up over my head. It got stuck over my eyes, the neckline struggling to expand over my forehead, but that was beside the point. I could feel it … yes … a cold wind was circling around my midriff … I'd done it. Take that, Meena Chandra. My top had come up with my jumper!'

'India Smythe!' came the booming voice across the rows and rows of students.

'Yes,' I replied, my voice muffled by the jumper that was still stuck over my head.

'Help her, will you, Meena Chandra.'

Meena tugged my jumper back down over my head.

'Please explain to the rest of us what on earth you are doing.'

Proving to my best friend that I wasn't inappropriately hitting on my tutor.

'I was hot,' I replied, shakily. 'So I was taking my jumper off.'

Mrs Trent's eyebrows shot so far up her head that they became part of her hairline.

'Hot? HOT?'

'Yes,' I replied.

'Then you should cool down. Please finish the rest of hymn practice outside. Leave the hall by the side door and if you stand on the other side of the glass fire doors, you'll still be able to read the words.

Was she serious? It was, like, minus two out there.

'I'm waiting.'

That'd be a 'yes' then.

I traipsed out of the hall and took my place on the other side of the glass doors. My teeth were chattering in my jaw and I tried to block out the hundreds of pairs of eyes that kept swivelling in my direction and the hundreds of mouths laughing at me.

Every now and then Mrs Trent would point in my direction and I had to make a big show of mouthing the words.

And did those feeeeeeeeeet in an-ci-ent tiiiiiimes.

I might be dying from hypothermia but at least I'd made my point. At least I'd próven that unintentional stomach flashes were a thing.

Finally hymn practice finished and I rejoined the others. I tried to wave at them but my hands were frozen little curled-up bird claws.

'You've gone blue,' remarked Anna, concerned. 'Shall I take you to the office?'

'No, I'm OK,' I stammered.

'You sure?' Meena asked.

'Admit it,' I said. 'Admit it's a thing.'

Meena paused. She hated being wrong. All the time I've known her she's never admitted to being wrong. At last that was about to change.

'It's not my fault you've got a weird skin condition that repels fabric.'

Seriously?

I've felt a bit weird all weekend. And not because of Rich, or my parents, or anything from school, which makes it even weirder.

On Saturday morning I read the weekly news magazine my parents get. They don't normally leave it out. They stuff it away somewhere out of sight as they're massively over-protective and don't want me to read anything unpleasant. 'There are things that go on in the world, India, that you don't need to know about.'

Anyway, maybe they'd had one too many glasses of wine last night, but they'd left their magazine on the sofa. When I wandered into the living room after breakfast I saw it there and thought I'd have a quick read. I was quite interested to see what all these monstrous goings-on were.

I didn't have to search hard. Pride of place, first page, an article: 'Coronavirus – a Global Emergency?'

What? What what-ty WHAT????

I read on. Words jumped around on the page.

Wuhan.

2,000 people infected.

Bats.

I tried to wake myself up to check this wasn't a dream. It did seem a bit like the plot of a movie and about 95% of my dreams tend to be movie-based 'This is a dream,' I said out loud and slapped my face. No. Apparently it wasn't. I was still in the living room. Still reading about a killer virus sweeping the globe.

How come this was the first I was hearing about this? None of my friends were talking about it. School hadn't mentioned it. My parents? My parents…

I stormed into the kitchen. Mum was with her Nespresso, Dad with his Nescafé.

They looked up at the sound of stomping feet.

I thrust the magazine in front of them.

'India, you shouldn't be reading that!' yelled Dad, snatching it from my hands.

'Really?' I shouted back. 'When exactly were you going to tell me about this virus then?'

'Oh, don't worry about that,' said Mum calmly. 'It won't come here.'

'That's not what this seems to be saying!'

'It'll be just the same as SARS and all the other ones. Everyone makes a big fuss but nothing actually happens. Not here anyway. This is the first new virus in the time of social media, that's all.'

Of course. It was the fault of smart phones. In Mum's mind *everything* was the fault of smart phones.

'And, India,' Dad added. 'We didn't want to tell you as we thought you'd overreact. Remember when you were little and our old neighbour told you there'd been something called bird flu? You wouldn't go to the duck pond for ages. You even refused to eat chicken nuggets for a month.'

'Andrew, I've never given her chicken nuggets,' shouted Mum angrily. 'Goujons maybe. But never *nuggets*.'

Great. She gets wound up about naming breaded chicken pieces, but say there's a killer virus and ... nothing?

'This seems a bit more serious than bird flu,' I snapped.

'It'll all blow over, India, you'll see,' said Mum, infuriatingly calm once more.

'But what about half term? Corfu? Should we really be getting on a plane? You've always said they're like disease incubators.'

'It's fine, India,' said Dad, the look of fire in his eyes saying everything. There was no way he was going to miss the shackling of his only single friend. 'We'll use hand sanitiser on the plane. I'll buy some Dettol spray.'

Monday.

At first break I asked the gang what they thought about the whole virus thing.

Meena and Gillian hadn't heard about it so at least I wasn't the only ignorant person in Surrey. Anna had heard about it, but thought we 'wouldn't be that interested in discussing it'.

'Why would you think that, Anna?' I asked, outraged.

'Sorry,' she replied. 'I just didn't think current affairs was your kind of thing.'

Me and Meena exchanged offended glances.

'It's so cool that we can talk about it though,' Anna continued. 'Do you think its mode of transmission is more likely to be that of the acute respiratory diseases like SARS in which a track and trace system would be the best method to contain it or do you think it will follow the pattern of a flu-variant in which case herd immunity is the only realistic option?'

Me:	Ummmmm.
Meena:	Ummmmm.
Gillian:	Ummmmm.

Maybe she'd been right in the first place.

There were ten minutes left of break so we headed to the library to see if there were some more magazines with information about it. I knew Mrs Greenwood kept some serious current affairs-style magazines in a rack by the window section.

We each picked a magazine and skimmed it for relevant information.

All of us had super-serious investigator faces on. All apart from Meena.

'Yes!' she cried, halfway through an article. 'They've shut schools! In China and South Korea they've actually shut schools!!'

She flashed the page in my face. The photo was of someone in a huge white suit that looked more like it was designed for a moon landing than anything else and a new hospital behind them that the caption said had been built in two days.

'And what you're taking away from this is that it's good they might close schools?!' I asked incredulously.

Meena nodded and grinned.

'You do realise if they shut schools we'll also be basically under house arrest and not be able to hang out and see each other?'

'Oh, I hadn't thought of that.'

Dear God.

The bell rang and French called. I wasn't ready. I wanted to chat about this virus a bit more. I was almost sad that the new extension had been finished and we weren't in the temporary classrooms outside any more. It meant Lisa could no longer lock Madame Higgins out of the lesson.

The week went by in a bit of a blur and before I realised it, it was Thursday again. Not only was there Netball Club, but this time we were actually playing a match. A 'friendly' against Rainston Girls.

Mum casually mentioned over breakfast that she might come to watch.

'Parents don't watch Netball Club,' I said firmly.

'Oh, if there're matches they do,' she replied confidently. I bumped into Gillian's Mum in Cup and Saucer yesterday and she said that lots of parents watch the matches.'

A curse on keen mums everywhere.

'Well, try not to call out or say anything,' I said earnestly. It was very important that she understood this. 'And try not to let April and Lisa see you.'

'Are they going to be there? I've got a good mind to—'

'*Muuuummm!*'

'OK, I won't say anything. Promise. See you later.'

I would have said see you later back but my mouth was too full of bagel.

Anyway, lessons dragged by. Lunch wasn't even much better. Anna wanted to talk about the virus, Meena wanted to act like she'd never heard about it and Gillian wanted to discuss netball tactics ready for the game later.

At one point I gave up and gazed off into the distance, trying to zone out of the noise.

'What are you thinking about?' Meena asked. Noise that asks you a direct question is pretty hard to ignore.

'Nothing.'

'If it's how you're going to break up with Rich, I can help.'

'I'M NOT GOING TO BREAK UP WITH RICH!'

'Really?'

'REALLY. You don't know anything about our relationship. We have a good time. A great time. I really like him. And I think I am definitely falling in love with him.'

Do I? Am I? I really didn't know but I wanted to wipe that smug look off Meena's face.

'OK, prove it,' Meena said, smug look unwiped.

'What do you mean?'

'Invite him out with us. Then we can see.'

'What do you mean you "can see"?'

'If you're in love with him.'

'I am.'

'Invite him out then and prove it.'

'Fine, I will.'

'This Saturday.'

'I only wish it could be sooner.'

'Great, looking forward to it.'

'Not as much as I am.'

I wasn't looking forward to it. Not even a little bit. It was going to be the most pressurised time I'd ever spent with Rich.

All in all, it was one of the worst lunch breaks I've ever had. I hope Rich isn't free on Saturday. It's Thursday already, after all, so he's probably got plans.

Anyway, when the final bell of the day rang I really wanted to go home and curl up on the sofa, but I couldn't. I had to head to the changing rooms. All because I'd stupidly said that I 'wanted to get fit' and 'didn't want to die young'.

Ms Hatchard bounced in as I was putting my trainers on.

'Right, girls. Rainston have just got here. They're warming up on the court so get your bibs on and get out there. We're going to tear them to pieces. We're going to crush them. Defence – stick to them like you're a mugger. Attack – I want you to be like pit bulls. Own the ball. Own the court. Make them beg for it and still don't give them a look in.'

I was horrified. If this was a 'friendly', what was a non-friendly? Did Ms Hatchard go all out and advocate cannibalism? *Tear them to pieces and then EAT THEM UP.* No one else seemed to be disturbed. Gillian was whooping and cheering. I took the Goal Keeper bib that had been thrust at me and followed the others onto the court. I had a feeling I wasn't going to enjoy this much.

And I was right.

Walking to my semicircle starting position I met my opposite number – Rainston's Goal Shooter. God, what did they feed her? She must have been at least six feet tall. Trying to guard her would be like a sheep trying to share tree leaves with a giraffe.

The whistle blew and the ball shot down towards my end of the court. Wing Attack à Goal Attack à pathetic attempt by me to intercept which ended up me falling flat on my face à Goal Shooter.

'Mark her, India,' came the less-than-supportive cry from Lisa as I dragged myself up to standing.

I reached as high as I could on tiptoes, my arms outstretched. They only came up to the Goal Shooter's collar bone. She aimed and the ball sailed through the hoop.

'Indiaaaaa!' Lisa again.

'You're supposed to support your teammates.' A new voice, from the sidelines. Oh no, no, no. Mum. Mum 'supporting' me in leggings and a too-short angora jumper. 'I think India tried really hard, and that's what counts.'

Lisa sniggered. Everyone sniggered.

The whistle blew again and pretty much the same thing happened as before apart from I didn't fall over this time. Apparently I'm as useless on my feet as I am on the ground.

This time the disappointed cry of 'Indiaaaa' came from outside the court. I looked to find its source. Rachel's mum. The keen one.

Mum was marching over, no doubt to set her straight. Oh God. I tried to lip-read what Mum was saying but she was too far away. And I have no idea how to lip-read.

Third attempt. Third time lucky. Wing Attack passed to Goal Attack. Goal Attack passed to Goal Shooter, or rather *tried* to pass to Goal Shooter. Somehow, my body got in the way. Somehow I was actually defending by accident. The ball hurtled towards my body and I panicked. (Which I think is a totally natural reaction. I'm sure all cavemen who didn't panic when a boulder shot in their direction got wiped out so if you think about it, panicking is an evolutionary survival trait.) Anyway, I panicked, so rather than catching the ball, as is traditional, I sort of chest-bumped it out the way. Straight into the hands of the Goal Shooter.

'Indiaaaaaaaa!' The word was being yelled at me from so many directions it was difficult to pinpoint its multiple origins. I turned to Ms Hatchard for support but saw her mouth was also open in an 'Indiaaaaaaaa' shape. Seems that there's one word I can lip-read. At least she had the grace to look a bit guilty when our eyes locked.

Then something good happened. Finally something good in this terrible day. I was heading back to my position for humiliation take four, when I managed to trip over my own foot and twisted my ankle. Properly twisted it. So I couldn't put any weight on it or anything.

'Owwww!' I exclaimed, sitting down.

'Are you OK?' asked the giraffe.

'Owww,' I said again, really just for consistency. To be honest, it stopped hurting as soon as I sat down, but if I admitted that, my first 'Ow' would have looked like a total over-reaction. It was best to double-down on the 'Ow's.

'Gillian, help India up,' called Ms Hatchard.

Gillian put her arm round me and I stood up, fine, but winced, possibly a bit too dramatically.

'Do you want to play on or leave the game?' Ms Hatchard barked.

'I think I'd better leave,' I said pathetically.

'Good idea,' replied Ms Hatchard, her face flooding with relief. How rude. There wasn't even a substitute. She thought her team would do better without me. That I was worse than nothing. 'And,' she continued, 'take as long as you need to recover. These things can take weeks, months even, to properly heal.'

Wow. I must be really bad. Really, really bad. Where was Ms Hatchard's concern for my shortened life expectancy now?

'Oh, OK,' I said, limping towards Mum.

I hadn't even left the court by the time Ms Hatchard blew the whistle and the game continued. Without me.

'Are you OK?' Mum asked as I finally reached her.

'I'll survive,' I said, the brave and wounded soldier.

'I thought so,' Mum said. 'You kept switching the leg you were limping on.'

Oh. Bit of a giveaway.

'Not that I mind,' Mum added. 'Nasty game, netball. 'No one shouts at each other like that in Pilates.'

Back home I texted Rich to see if he was free Saturday night. Annoyingly he was. And seemed quite excited to come out with my friends. The fool.

'Where shall we meet? x' I asked.

'Yours x' came the reply.

I felt all warm and fuzzy inside. He wanted to pick me up from my house even though it was completely out of his way.

'I'm finishing band practice with your Dad at around 7 so see you outside your garage then? x'

And the warm fuzzy feeling was gone.

Saturday evening. I took ridiculously long to decide what to wear. How to most look like someone definitely in love…? We were all going to the cinema so dressing up too much would have seemed weird and desperate, but if I made no effort at all, then Meena would say it was because I just saw Rich as a friend and nothing more.

After multiple outfit changes I ended up where I'd started, in tight jeans and a black top, with mascara AND eyeliner, just to show I was trying. I surveyed myself in the mirror. Yes, I looked like someone going on a date. Someone who might well be in love with the person they were going on a date with.

I said goodbye to Mum and then hovered around

outside the garage door, waiting for the guitar chords and cello strings to recede.

Finally Rich emerged, cheeks red and hair plastered down his forehead.

'Hey,' he smiled, bending down to kiss me. The skin above his top lip was clammy. 'Sorry,' he said. 'It gets a bit hot in your garage.'

'You can stop, you know. I'll tell Mum she has to make Dad leave your band. She'll do it if I pick the right moment.'

'Errr…' Rich hesitated. Why was he hesitating? I was offering him the gift of freedom. What was there to 'errr' about? 'Actually,' he continued, 'your Dad's quite a good guitarist and he was … you know … kind of right. Guitar was the sound we were missing.'

Oh. My. God. Rich now actually *wanted* Dad in his band. Maybe that was why he was going out with me? Maybe Meena was right… maybe Rich wasn't that into me, he just couldn't dump me because that would mean he'd lose Dad and his 'sweet chords'???

It was too terrible to think about. And there was also no time to think about it. We were supposed to be meeting the gang in Rainston in twenty-five minutes and Rich was all sweaty and definitely didn't look like he'd made enough effort. He might secretly want to dump me but tonight he had to look like he was very much in love with me and make Meena eat her words.

I took a tissue from my bag.

'Here, let me,' I said, and started dabbing his face. His face that was wearing a slightly surprised expression.

'What are you doing?' he asked. I had moved on from the face now. Dabbing and tousling his hair. It was a fine balance between matted down (no effort, Rich doesn't love India) and curled up (too much forehead, India doesn't love Rich).

'Can you … err… stop, please?'

'Sure,' I said, stepping back and surveying my work. Not. Too. Shabby.

Meena and Anna were already outside the cinema. Gillian had bailed. There was a last-minute opportunity to play some floodlit hockey.

Meena had chosen the film: *Gretel and Hansel*. I didn't know anything about it, but she insisted it was the best movie on and the only one we didn't need fake ID in order to watch.

Rich offered to buy popcorn for everyone, which was massively generous as it's so expensive in the cinema. We normally just sneak in sweets instead. Rich said he'd got some money for helping his neighbours load their things into a removal van.

'See,' said the look I shot Meena. Kind. Generous. Strong and Muscular. The perfect boyfriend. Who I am in love with.

Meena rolled her eyes.

We went to sit down. Anna sat closest in. I sat next to Anna, then Rich sat next to me (obviously), and Meena was at the end. Meena didn't even pretend to face the screen. She just sat there, staring intently at me and Rich, analysing our every interaction. The pressure was on. I put my hand on Rich's arm but at the same time he lifted it up to get some more popcorn so it looked like he was brushing it off. Meena grinned. One point to her. I had to even the score. What to do … what to do… Hand on leg. That was it. Friends don't go around putting their hands on each other's legs. That was definitely a romantic manoeuvre. I put my left hand down. Squeezing his thigh as only a girlfriend might. But … oh God … oh no … I aimed too high. That definitely wasn't his thigh. Rich gave a squeal and chucked all his popcorn in the air. In rained down on us like confetti while Meena had hysterics and I wanted to crawl into a corner and die.

'Is everything OK?' Rich leant over and whispered to me. 'You're acting a bit strange.'

'Everything's fine,' I said in a weird, strangled voice.

I don't know if the film was any good. I didn't watch it. The images flashed in front of my eyes but they weren't focusing.

We went for ice cream afterwards. Anna's suggestion.

There's an ice cream café halfway up the High Street that stays open late at weekends. I ordered chocolate brownie flavour reckoning that the worst a massive sugar hit could do was restore my energy levels and confidence to minus fifty. Rich sat next to me, but not super-close. Like he was leaving a safety barrier in case I chose to pounce on him again.

'So what did you think of the film?' Anna asked.

'Yeah, OK,' Rich said.

'Did you think it was romantic?' Meena asked, staring directly at Rich.

'Um … errr … no, not really. It was a sort of horror film, wasn't it?' Rich looked flustered. The pink was beginning to return to his cheeks.

'What do you think is romantic then?' persevered Meena. 'Paris or a water park?'

'Right … er … well. Paris is supposed to be lovely. But to be honest, I think I'd prefer to go to a water park.'

Meena did her most annoying knowing look.

'And,' she added, 'just for the record – what is your personal view on chipmunks?'

Rich threw me a 'help!' look and I shut Meena down and told her it was time for me and Rich to head.

We walked together to the bus stop.

It was awkward between us. The first time it's ever been properly awkward.

'Thanks for coming out with my friends,' I said.

'That's OK.' Rich's voice sounded anything but OK. There was a pause before he spoke again. 'I'm not sure they liked me though. They kept asking very weird questions.'

'It's because of a stupid survey,' I said, and then regretted it as soon as the words were out of my mouth.

'What survey?'

'A survey to see if we were…' *don't say in love, don't say in love*, 'compatible.' *Nice save.*

'And were we?'

I thought about it. We did both like water parks. I'm pretty sure if I pressed him, Rich would be a fan of chipmunks. When it came down to it, we were pretty compatible.

'I guess so,' I said and grinned.

He grinned back and put his arm round me. I nuzzled in. I thought for a moment.

'Why didn't you put your arm round me when we were with my friends?' I asked.

'I thought it'd be a bit off,' he said. 'I mean they don't have boyfriends. I didn't want to rub it in their faces how much I like you.'

He grinned again, deepening his dimples, and his cheeks tinged pink.

'I really like you too,' I said, grinning back at him.

180

Sunday.

I woke with a smile on my face. I liked Rich Evans and Rich Evans liked me. It was suddenly crystal clear that that was all that mattered. Was I in love with him? Was he in love with me? It didn't matter. We didn't have to be at that stage yet. We were just two people who really liked each other and shared a mutual interest in water parks (and very probably chipmunks). And that was OK by me.

I texted Meena to tell her so and she actually sent something nice back:

'Cool. Say thanks for the popcorn x'

But what should have been a great day was then marred for two reasons.

Reason number 1: My Dad invited the new neighbours from across the street round for coffee to 'get to know them better'/work out what exactly to tell MI5.

Cheekbones-Dave and Pete-the-child didn't come, thank God, so I thought I could go and hide in my room after a token 'hello'. There's nothing worse than being forced into awkward social situations with randoms you're expected to get on with just because you were born in the same decade. It doesn't happen later in life.

I doubt anyone's going, 'Nancy, you have to meet Clive. You're both in your fifties. You'll have loads to talk about.'

I still didn't escape completely unscathed though. Before I ran away, Dad made me pass round a plate of biscuits.

'Just shortbread, I'm afraid. We don't have any *caviar*, sorry,' he said, staring closely, mental reporter's notebook ready to jot down Sheila, the mum's reaction. Would she crumple, knowing Dad had rumbled her cover? Nope. If they are Russian agents, they are trained very well as Sheila just looked thoroughly weirded out.

'Biscuits will do just fine, thanks,' *you strange, strange man.*

Dad wasn't defeated.

'Tell me again, what part of Russia are you from?'

Jim, Sheila's husband, choked on his shortbread.

'Not Russia,' Sheila said through gritted teeth. 'We've never been to Russia. As I said, we're from Kent originally. Well, I'm from Kent. Jim's from Hampshire.' I got the impression this wasn't the first time Dad had asked this question.

Mum shot daggers at Dad. She clearly wasn't on board with the whole Russian undercover spy thing. Probably because she only watched season one of *The Americans*.

'And what is it you both do?' she asked, trying to steer the conversation towards more neutral ground.

'We're actually both travel agents,' Sheila replied, perking up a bit. 'We run a travel agency together.'

A sort of strangled, muffled version of 'A-ha!' escaped Dad's lips. While I was thinking whether I needed to call for professional help, I remembered: the Russian couple in *The Americans* ran a travel agency. Together. In Dad's mind it was *case closed, Your Honour.*

As Sheila and Jim started backing away towards the door, Mum flew into action. She grabbed the plate of biscuits from me and stood, blocking their path.

'Another piece of shortbread?' she said, a steely look in her eye. 'It's homemade.' She was going to buy herself time to restore our reputation. There was no way she was letting these people head out into the street and tell everyone what a bunch of nutters lived at number 51.

'Isn't it a good year for hellebores?' she continued, taking Sheila forcibly by the arm and frog marching her to the back window to stare at the garden. 'And there's such a variety available now. I was at the garden centre the other day and I found it really hard to choose between the Merlins and the Penny's Pinks. In the end I chose the Penny's Pinks … there … yes, beneath the magnolia. I love their marbled foliage.'

Well, our reputation was destroyed anyway. If we

weren't the nutters at number 51, we were the most boring people in the world at number 51.

But … Sheila was actually smiling. And nodding. Jim was even coming over to have a look. God, what is it with old people and plants?!

They chatted a bit more about hellebores then riffed on snowdrops before bigging up daffodils. It was dire. Then the conversation changed. Thank God, I thought. Until I actually heard what was being said.

'Seems like our Pete has taken a bit of a shine to your India,' Sheila said, smiling. As if it was entirely acceptable and appropriate and he might stand half a chance.

I spluttered on my tea as Mum joined in with a 'young love'.

Feeling thoroughly disgusted I climbed the stairs to distance myself from these people. My parents' bedroom door was open and on their bed I spotted…

Reason 2: Their Sunday paper.

The headline read: 'WHO Declares Coronavirus a Global Health Emergency.'

I skim-read the article. The virus wasn't just in China. It was now in at least eighteen countries. It was … in the UK!!!!!!!!! Two Chinese nationals had fallen ill with it in a hotel in York. This was terrible. This was more than terrible. And why exactly had my parents not mentioned this to me? I take a week off from reading articles in the school library because they get a bit scary (and boring) and this happens.

As soon as I heard the front door open and the Russians/Sheila and Jim leave, I stormed downstairs, newspaper in hand. I pointed accusatorially at the headline.

Mum: Oh, India, we didn't want to worry you.
Dad: We knew you'd overreact. You always do.

Spoken completely non-ironically by the spymaster general himself.

They tried to reassure me, but failed dismally. Not least because Dad let slip that we're no longer going to Corfu at half term as Kev decided it might not be the *best time to fly at the moment*. Why not? If everything's really so OK, we could get on a plane, right? So everything is clearly NOT so OK.

'Don't worry, the wedding's still on,' Dad said, as if that was my major concern. 'It's just been moved. Somewhere south of Crawley. That man is getting tied down.'

And a smile spread over Dad's lips. The world might be going to hell, but his oldest friend was still losing his freedom so everything was OK.

My family is really messed up.

School's got hand sanitiser now. A huge pump thing of it is perched on the reception desk. It might not seem like a big deal but it somehow is. School has always been, like, the most unhygienic place on earth. The soap dispensers in the toilets are often empty, the glass doors have finger marks on them and Lucy Brennan, who has school lunch, once said she found three different coloured hairs in her lasagne.

The teachers have also decided we no longer shake or otherwise touch hands with them. Not that our form teacher, Mrs Johnson, was previously a massive high-fiver. Or shaker. A cold, tight claw grip at the end of each term was the most she was ever comfortable with. Other classes with nicer form teachers get to invent their own handshake equivalents. 10F are touching shoes together. 10B bump elbows. 10E even do the funky chicken dance. It must take ages for Ms Eaton to dismiss the whole class.

We also had a whole-year talk about social distancing and coughing today. They've abandoned whole-school assemblies as they've realised that stuffing us in like sardines isn't the best idea. Maybe this means hymn practice will stop as well. Silver linings… Today's talk was led by the Deputy Head of Sixth Form, Miss Hendricks, who is mousy and terrified of non-sixth form students. In her quavering introduction, the clicker shaking in her right hand, she told us that before she became a teacher 'years ago', she was head of communications at a big City Firm, which is why she was chosen to speak to us today. She was terrible. I can only imagine the firm must have fired her which is why she became a teacher. She decided to 'spice up' her presentation with lots of videos and pictures. If you can say it with a GIF…

She pointed the wobbling clicker at the screen and click…

A video started about a hedgehog realising he could show he liked someone without hugging them…

Hedgehog gave a wave to Mole and Mole waved back.

Hedgehog then did a little dance to Rat. Rat danced back.

They were still friends.

(Obligatory rainbow.)

The hall was filled with peals of laughter. It was a terrible, terrible choice of video. Never show something to Year 10s that is aimed at Year 1s. And, huge logical flaw – no one would have hugged a hedgehog in the first place. No surprise that Mole and Rat were smiling. They were smiling because they no longer had to get holes pierced into them every time they said 'hello'.

Then Miss Hendricks, now even more nervous and agitated, started talking about coughing. About how you had to cover your mouth rather than spray saliva everywhere – *really?* – but also how you shouldn't cough into your hand but cough into your elbow instead.

'Cough like Batman!' she said, pressing play on a matching GIF and looking round the hall waiting for the congratulatory laughter that never came. It was all very embarrassing and prompted lots of fake coughing around the hall.

'Silence!' Mrs Johnson leapt onto the stage. She'd witnessed enough and, realising Miss Hendricks was out of her depth, had decided to take charge.

'Anyone coughing will receive a detention,' she snapped.

The coughing stopped immediately.

Mrs Johnson then picked up the clicker and sped through the rest of Miss Hendricks' presentation.

'Wash your hands for twenty seconds… It says here to sing *Happy Birthday* twice in your head. I think that's entirely unnecessary. You all do maths. You can count. Count to twenty, none of this namby-pamby rubbish.'

She flicked through the remaining slides.

'No, nothing else important here.'

Miss Hendricks' face fell to see her work dissed like this.

Mrs Johnson didn't notice. Or more likely, she noticed and didn't care.

'Year 10 dismissed,' she barked. 'Leave the hall silently. And remember: coughing means detention.'

Meena poked me as we walked down the corridor, back to class.

'Cough like Batman,' she whispered, elbow over her mouth, eyes fixed in a superhero intense glare.

I laughed but the fear had started to build again. The teachers were being hideously embarrassing as always, but what they were talking about was real.

The virus was real and I didn't want it to be.

Rich surprised me after school. I hadn't arranged to meet him or anything but he must have got out early for some reason and was standing, a bit sheepishly, some metres away from the St Mary's gate. I was so pleased to see him that I nearly skipped over. Luckily I didn't. My leg only managed a little bounce before the self-preservation section of my brain shut it down.

'Hey,' he smiled. 'I've got something for you.'

He held out an envelope.

Hmmm. What could it be? Nothing good comes in envelopes. Well, that's not quite true. At Christmas, cash from elderly relatives I've hardly met sometimes comes in envelopes, but I'm not sure I'd feel entirely great about myself and our relationship if Rich handed me an envelope stuffed with cash.

I opened it. No cash. Phew. Instead there was a piece of printed card. On one side was a black and white image of a couple – two faces staring longingly at each other. I turned it over to see the words:

Intense: a photographic expression of the stages of love.

Then there were details in smaller print.

'It's Mum's exhibition,' Rich explained. 'Please say you can come. She gets really intense – no pun intended – when she's got a show on, so it'd be really good to have you there.'

I looked at the date. 13th March. A Friday.

'That should be fine,' I said. I still couldn't believe it. A photo of *me* was going to be in a prestigious London show!

I checked the location.

Oh.

A photo of me was going to be in a show in Rainston Town Hall. But it was still something. Something pretty cool.

'And Mum said to tell you that your friends are obviously welcome and your parents are invited too.'

'Hahahahahaha,' I laughed. There was no way my parents were coming to look at an Intense exhibition that included a photo of me and Rich in love.

'OK, but I promised my mum I'd ask. She kind of wanted to meet them seeing that things are … a bit … that we're quite … you know.'

I think I did know. I'd got myself a great guy.

But that didn't change things. There was no way my parents were coming to the exhibition.

'What's this invite?' Mum flounced into breakfast brandishing the invite from Rich's mum. 'I found it on your desk. It looks very *adult*.'

'You shouldn't have been going through my desk!' I squealed. *Is nothing sacrosanct?*

'It was *on* your desk. I was *hardly* going through it!'

'You shouldn't have been looking at my stuff, though!'

'I won't need to look at your stuff if you actually start tidying your room! It's a pigsty – I can't find anything.'

'You don't need to find anything. It's *my* room!'

Aggghhhh.

'Anyway, you still haven't answered my question. Why do you have this invite?'

I sighed. There was no way round this.

'Rich's mum is having an exhibition. One of the photos is of me and Rich.'

Dad snapped his book shut and sat up dead straight like a meerkat.

'She's taken an *adult* photo of you and Rich and is putting it in a *show*!' His voice had gone from baritone to an indignant soprano squeal in under ten seconds.

'NO!' I shouted back, before he had a heart attack. 'There's just a photo of me sitting next to Rich. That's all.'

'Are all your clothes on?'

'Dad!'

'Are they?'

'Yes!'

'Are you kissing him?'

'No!'

'Are you sure?'

'YES!'

'OK, we'll come then. Samantha, write it on the calendar.'

What? I didn't invite them. They were never invited. But there was nothing I could do. The trouble is they *had* been invited. I couldn't even tell them they couldn't come as Dad would just ask Rich and Rich would confess all as he's terrified of Dad.

It's a few weeks away, I told myself.

They'll probably forget.

Later that morning I tried to rub out the calendar entry. Didn't work. Mum had written it in Sharpie.

The days leading up to half term felt weirder and weirder. It was hard to put my finger on what was different exactly, but everyone was a little bit on edge.

For a start, Meena was being over-sincerely nice.

'I'll definitely come to the show,' she said. 'And I'm sorry I was weird about Rich before. I think I was just a bit jealous, you know. Because you have a boyfriend and everything and I … well, I don't yet.'

She'd just done what she never does – admit she'd been in the wrong. And apologised. It freaked me out.

'I was as bad,' I replied, truthfully. 'I kept on making a massive deal about being in love and everything.'

Now, normal Meena would have gone – *hahahahaha – yes you were worse.* But this Meena didn't. She just smiled beatifically. Like the Virgin Mary herself.

'What's going on?' I asked.

'I just wanted to make my peace with you in case this virus, you know…'

'What?'

'Wipes us all out.'

Great. Absolutely brilliant.

Mum and Dad were being weird as well.

Mum's become a hoarder. I went to get my raincoat from the understairs cupboard but could hardly get inside as my path was blocked by tower upon tower of loo roll. It was like loo roll Jenga.

'Just in case,' she said. 'It'll be the first thing to go.'

And Dad. Dad's started hoarding too. Just in a less effectual way. He came back from the shops with normal food plus three tins of Big Soup.

'Just in case,' he said, nodding sagely.

In case what? We feel hungry one mealtime? How exactly are three tins of Big Soup going to make any practical difference come the apocalypse?!

One night I even heard them talking about where they'd go if it all kicked off and Britain suddenly went proper dystopian. Dad's favourite book is *The Death of Grass* and in it apparently they go and take over some remote valley. Dad was even talking about stealing Mr Green from number 32's boat to start our escape by river. I think that's really because he can't stand Mr Green and has been complaining for ages about him parking his 'rusty old piece of garbage' on his front drive.

'Serve him right,' Dad chuckled.

Finally half term came and it was a relief to flee school. It always is, but this was relief plus (the added sugar and caffeine variety). Mrs Johnson handed us a sheet of paper for us to read over half term. I glanced at it. The basic message was: if you feel even a tiny bit ill, STAY AWAY, you disgusting, probably virus-ridden diseased person.

And happy half term to you too.

Everything had got so weird that I was actually pleased when it came time to pack to go to Kev's wedding.

The venue was only about forty-five-minutes' drive away but I think Mum and Dad planned to get wasted as they'd booked us into a Premier Inn within staggering distance from the reception. To be honest, I was pretty pleased because, as much as the idea of sharing a room with my parents repulses me, Premier Inns have amazing buffet breakfasts.

We got into our smart clothes at home. Mum had wanted to change at the hotel as she was worried about the drive creasing her dress, but Dad and I had both insisted on getting dressed here instead as there was no way we were changing in the same room. Plus, it would have meant that I got changed in the Premier Inn bathroom where the lighting is more strip light than soft diffused bulbs so I would have looked horrific and locked myself in and never come out again.

I wore the green dress that Mum had bought me for Lisa's Christmas Party and kept having flashbacks to that terrible evening. I thought about swapping but I had no other winter dresses and there was no way Mum was going to rush to the shops and spend more money on me.

Mum wore a lacy beige dress and far-too-pink lipstick and Dad squeezed himself into a far-too-small tux.

'Can you believe I still fit into this from our wedding?' he said proudly, only managing to do up one set of buttons, before going to kiss Mum who pushed him away in case he smudged her lipstick.

The drive over was quite tense.

'We'll be the first people there, we're bound to be,' Mum said. 'Kev is just so disorganised… I can't believe he's got someone to agree to marry him. Such an unstable lifestyle being in a band.'

'Yes,' Dad agreed. But I could see the wistful expression in his eyes reflected in the rear-view mirror.

The wedding invite said 3pm and when we pitched up at 3:15pm the church was already full.

'Oh,' said Mum.

Kev was standing at the front. It was like he'd had an extreme makeover. His long hair and terrible leather jacket were gone. Instead he had cropped hair, a neat beard and a tailored light grey suit. He looked almost handsome for an old person.

'Oh,' said Mum again.

One of Dad's other ex-bandmates, Liam, scuttled down the aisle to say 'hi'.

'Have you heard about Kev's record deal?' he said. 'He's just been given a huge advance for an acoustic album.'

'Oh,' said Dad.

Next thing, the music started and in walked Kev's bride-to-be, Susie. She wore a long tight-fitting white silk dress and was smiling. She was max twenty-five.

'Oh,' said Dad again.

'Gold-digger,' Mum whispered.

'Yes,' Dad agreed.

The vicar wasn't too bad and he sped through it all quite quickly, but for once I didn't even mind. Mum and Dad were wrong. The couple, Kev and Susie, they looked so in love. He just obviously totally adored her and she adored him too. I wanted that. To have someone love me that much and to love them back.

As we headed to the reception in a marquee nearby, Mum whispered to Dad, 'She is very pretty, isn't she?'

For once Dad realised he was standing in a minefield. Deny, and he's obviously lying. Agree, and he's basically said he wants an affair.

'She is very pretty,' Dad said carefully, 'but it is hard for me to judge as my wife is the most beautiful woman in the world.'

'Oh, Andy,' Mum cooed. She then paused for a moment. 'I'm sorry if I made you give up the band.'

'No. Don't be. I've got you. I've got India. I'm a lucky guy.'

'Oh, Andy,' Mum said again and kissed him, lipstick be damned.

I guess they love each other too, in their own way.

The seating plans were up on a board as we entered the marquee. Damn. I wasn't with Mum and Dad. I was on my own. On the children's table.

'See you later, India,' Mum said vaguely. She was too busy nuzzling into Dad's shoulder. There was already a bright pink stain on his shirt collar. It was totally embarrassing. They seem to have forgotten they were in public.

I headed over to table 'Thunder Road' (they were all named after Springsteen songs) and stared at the place names. I was between an Archie and a Ryan. Ryan arrived next. He was about nine. Great. His opening question was whether I liked Minecraft. No hot men for India then.

'Hi, sorry … could I move your chair slightly?' There was a voice to my left. A soft sexy voice, coming from … a very fit face.

'Um … yeah … sure.' Less soft and sexy coming from my slightly panicked, flushed face.

'I'm Archie,' he said.

'India,' I replied.

'I'm one of Susie's cousins,' he drawled. 'How did you get roped in?'

'My Dad and Kev used to be bandmates. And my Mum used to date Kev.'

'Oh, very droll.'

The sexy voice and delivery was beginning to grate. It was the sort of self-assurance of someone who might one day become a tutor.

And it grated more and more as dinner went on.

He was obviously really hot. Objectively far hotter than Rich, but I began missing Rich. Missing him so much. He might be awkward. His forehead might be a tiny bit too high. OK, a lot too high. But he was real. And he made me laugh while I hadn't laughed at all this evening.

Finally, desserts came and a waitress stuck a plate in front of me with something that looked like custard and an uncooked meringue on. I eyed it suspiciously.

'Île Flottante,' Archie said knowingly. 'I had it once at this wonderful little bistro in Paris.'

I didn't react.

'Have you ever been to Paris, India?'

'No,' I replied. 'I'm more of a water park girl myself.'

'Oh I love water parks,' came this little squeaking voice from Minecraft-Ryan to my right. So I spent the rest of the evening talking to him, debating the advantages and disadvantages of rides with tyres as opposed to double floats as opposed to old-school bums on flumes.

As predicted, Mum and Dad were in no state to drive when the wedding wrapped at midnight. They couldn't even walk to the Premier Inn. We had to get an Uber the five minutes down the road. As they crawled into bed –

the bed next to mine – I heard Mum whisper, 'Oh, I wish India wasn't here right now,' and my toes curled and I felt physically sick.

I lay there in bed, still awake long after they'd fallen asleep, listening to Dad's rhythmic snoring and I realised something.

I don't just like Rich Evans. I love him. As in really love him.

So what do I do about that then?

The first few days of half term dragged. On Monday I expected Mum to offer to take me and a friend up to London. We normally do this sort of thing in half terms. I look round the shops and stuff and then meet up with her for lunch. She says she likes showing me off to her workmates. I think the truth is probably that it gives her an excuse to have a much longer lunch break than normal. This Monday – no offer came. Instead, she said she was going to try to work at home a bit more.

'Why?' I asked.

She and Dad exchanged glances.

'No reason,' she said.

The virus. Everything's about the virus.

By Tuesday I was so bored that when Pete-the-child rang on the bell to ask if I fancied 'hanging out' (*knowing wink*) I almost said 'yes'. Almost.

On Wednesday I met up with Meena and the gang in Rainston. We didn't go anywhere or do anything. We just hung out on a bench in the cold by the river watching a bunch of angry swans try to mug passers-by for bread.

'So,' I said as Meena finished a long story about how she'd realised she needed to go up a bra size after her left nipple kept popping out, 'I am in love with Rich Evans.'

'Not this again!' said Meena.

'No, for real this time. I do actually love him. So … do I tell him?'

A moment of silence then everyone weighed in at once.

Meena:	Of course you don't tell him. Boys are supposed to say it first. Period.
Anna:	Yes. If you love him that seems like a very sensible thing to do.
Gillian:	I don't care.

Enlightening as always.

But I had no one else to ask. Taking a deep breath,

my biggest fear spilled out of my mouth without my even meaning to share it.

Me: What if I say it and he doesn't say it back?
Meena: Then it's over. Obviously.
Anna: I guess you just wait till he feels the same.

Hmmm. Neither of these seemed like good options. I didn't want it to be over.

I didn't want to hang around hoping he would grow to love me back.

We walked back towards the shops to help Meena choose a bigger bra. She ended up going for a purple one with little white daisies on. All I could do was stare at the petals.

He loves me.

He loves me not.

Friday.

I saw Rich. He picked me up with a backpack on and said he was taking me for a picnic.

I looked up at the grey sky and he laughed and said, 'I've brought soup.'

He really was my perfect guy.

Anyway, we walked out of town, out towards the nature reserve and into the woods. He seemed to know where he was going.

'We're going to reach this glade soon,' he said. 'It's really beautiful. I've been wanting to show you for ages.'

He held my hand.

'I think it's just round this corner … just a couple more minutes… Oh…'

We rounded the corner and walked into a big gravel car park.

'Think I took a wrong turning somewhere,' he said quietly, 'sorry.'

Then we both started laughing.

'Are you hungry?' he asked.

'Starving,' I replied. So we sat on a bench at the edge of the car park and shared some cream of tomato soup and a ham roll. It was somehow impossibly romantic.

I glanced over at him. He was looking back at me, smiling.

'What?' he said eventually.

This was the moment, the perfect moment to tell him how I felt.

'Rich…'

He stared into my eyes.

'Yes?'

I stared into his.

'I love…'

'Yes…?'

'…cream of tomato soup.'

'Oh… Right… Me too.'

I love cream of tomato soup?! I love cream of tomato soup?! I'd had the perfect opportunity and I'd panicked and blown it.

Sunday.

Quick emergency meeting with the gang at Gillian's. I'd never actually been to Gillian's flat before. Her parents were out but we still went straight to her room as it somehow seemed more private. Predictably all the walls were covered with pictures of her sporting heroes. I hardly recognised anyone.

World Book Day was coming up so we were there to talk outfits. Dressing up was compulsory. The teachers always went high-end literature to show off what great readers they were. There were always at least two Miss Havishams. As a student it was trickier. You wanted to be somebody everyone recognised or you'd have to spend the whole day telling people who you were.

Nearly everyone just dressed up as TV and film characters, hoping that at some time there'd been a book it was based on. There usually was. And hardly anyone made their own costumes, they just bought something from Amazon and then the prize for best costume invariably went to whoever's parents spent the most money.

'What a wonderful Mary Poppins outfit!' Price tag £50.

Mum refuses to buy outfits from Amazon. 'Not more disposable PLAHstic that will kill the dolphins.' So I have to make mine.

This year I've managed to persuade Meena, Anna and Gillian to go with me as a sort of group ensemble. Safety in numbers and all that.

The question was what to go as?

Meena: Pretty Little Liars. There are four girls. We are
         four girls. Easy.
Me: That's a TV show.
Anna: (*Searching on her phone*) Apparently it was a
         book first.
Me: Oh. But still – no way.

What Meena totally failed to grasp was that the four girls in *Pretty Little Liars* are all supposed to be stunning.

Our motley crew couldn't go as Pretty Little Liars. Meena might be able to get away with it, but me, Anna and Gillian couldn't. No one in *Pretty Little Liars* wore a fleece, had a monobrow or had weird bobbly skin on their arms. No one would get who we were supposed to be and then we'd have to explain and everyone would think we were hilariously arrogant.

We needed another approach entirely.

Gillian: How about great sportswomen through the years?

Me: That's not a book.

Gillian: Yes it is.

She pulled a book called *Great Sportswomen Throughout the Years* off her shelf. It was nearly falling apart she'd read it so many times.

Gillian: We could be Casey Stoney, Debbie Jevans, Jessica Ennis-Hill and Chrissie Wellington.

Meena: No.

Me: No.

Anna: No.

I had literally no idea who any of those people were. Plus I wasn't going to dress up in front of the whole school in tight Lycra, which I assume is what great sportswomen wear.

Anna: If we can do non-fiction, how about influential female scientists?

Me: No. We can't do non-fiction. We need to be people from a book that normal people read. Preferably a book that's been made into a film.

Meena: How about we all go as people from The Hunger Games?

Hmmm. Not a terrible suggestion. At least everyone knows *The Hunger Games*.

Me: What are you thinking?

Meena: It'd be easy. We could be fighters from different districts. One of us, me, could have a bow and be Katniss. Someone else could have a net and be from the fishing district. Someone could have a spear. And someone could have an axe.

Me: I'm not sure there was an axe.

Meena: There was definitely an axe.

Me: OK.

Meena: So? How about it?

We all agreed. It seemed doable at least. Costumes were minimal, Anna and Gillian didn't have to wear dresses and I didn't have to wear Lycra so we were all good.

Meena got to be Katniss (typical) because she claimed (pretty dubiously) that she was 'really good at making bows'.

'Who's got a net?' Meena, our self-appointed leader, asked.

'Me,' I said.

'It's got to be big,' said Meena doubtfully. 'The sort of net you could catch someone in to stab them. Not a rubbishy rock-pooling net.'

'I *know*. We've got this big net Mum always uses to cover the plum tree in summer to stop the pigeons eating the fruit. It'd be perfect.'

'OK. Great. That just leaves the spear and the axe. Who's got plastic ones of those?'

Anna said her brother had a fake spear at home left over from when he was a Roman soldier in a play a few years ago.

Which left Gillian with the axe.

'No problem,' she said.

As we left Gillian's, Meena asked me, 'Did you tell him?'

'Nearly,' I replied.

She raised an eyebrow.

'I told him I love cream of tomato soup.'

She burst out laughing and gave me a hug.

'You're an idiot, you know.'

'I know.'

Monday. First day back.

Mrs Johnson was doing the register.

She got to Amy Roland's name. Silence. I looked around the class. No sign of her.

Kimberley Torban piped up, 'She's self-isolating at home, Miss. She went to Italy at half term so her mum is keeping her at home just in case.'

Mrs Johnson's eyebrows shot to the top of her forehead.

'Italy? At half term? In this situation? How perfectly ridiculous!'

Seems like Amy Roland is in for a double detention when she gets back. In Mrs Johnson's twisted mind, travelling to Italy at half term must be at least twice as bad as coughing.

It was strange though, to hear of someone self-isolating. From our school. It meant that the whole thing had just got a bit closer to home and a bit scarier.

At night I asked Mum about what was going on in Italy. I'd meant to go to the library at lunchtime to look at the news section but then I'd sort of chickened out.

'Nothing, love,' Mum said. 'Nothing for you to worry about, anyway.'

It even felt weird when I saw Rich for around five minutes after school for a quick snog. All I could think about was that my potentially germ ridden saliva was mixing with his potentially germ ridden saliva and that is not a very sexy thought.

World Book Day

Normally I'd have been waking up early, anxious about my outfit. This year, however, I was pretty relaxed. Up at seven. Plenty of time to put on black jeans and a black top (I think a tribute could probably wear that) and then head to the garden shed for the net. But, when I got there, the net … was gone. Fear started to rise. My whole outfit was based around this net. Where the hell was the net?!

'Mum!!!' I yelled.

She came sprinting down the garden towards me.

'Oh,' she said, as she skidded to a halt. 'I thought

you'd cut off a finger or something, you were making so much noise.'

Sorry to disappoint you with my non-mutilated body.

It turned out that the net had had a hole pecked in it by a particularly aggressive and hungry pigeon at the end of last summer and Mum had thrown it away. She'd thrown my World Book Day outfit in the bin.

'Don't worry. I'm sure we can find something else you can use,' she said, taking in my distraught face.

Mum rummaged deeper into the shed, pulled something out and then re-emerged with a triumphant smile on her face.

'Like this!'

She held up a kid's fishing net. The sort you might find in the hand of a rock-pooling five-year-old.

'It's not that sort of net!' I cried.

'Really?' she replied, miming fishing. 'I think you could catch something in this. On the small side probably. A shrimp maybe. But it would still work.'

'It's not supposed to be for catching shrimp! It's supposed to be for throwing over someone so I can bundle them up and stab them!'

'India! That is horrible! And completely inappropriate. I think you should go as something different. I know! I've an old white dress somewhere... Why don't you go as Miss Havisham?'

Agghhhh.

I took the fishing net and stormed out of the shed.

I met the rest of the gang just inside the school gate. Meena looked amazing. She'd already whipped off her jumper to reveal a tight, low-cut top and leggings and had a bow slung over her shoulder that she'd made from a bendy stick and some string. She was right. She was actually pretty good at making bows. Anna was in a fleece and carried a plastic spear. Gillian… Gillian was just in jeans and a top.

'Where's the axe?' I asked.

'Not this again,' Gillian sighed.

'What?' I said.

'Mr Parkinson confiscated it,' Meena explained.

'Why?'

'It was a real axe. Gillian brought a huge, metal axe to school.'

'Yeah,' admitted Gillian. 'It was an awesome axe. Cuts through wood like it's butter. I've got to go and see the head in a few minutes.'

Oh. My. God.

'What about you?' Meena asked. 'Where's the net?'

I sheepishly pulled the fishing net out from behind my back.

'Oh,' she said.

'Yeah, sorry.'

Meena sort of disowned us for the rest of the day so it was me with a fishing net, Anna with a plastic spear and Gillian with nothing, having to explain again and again to confused faces that we were tributes from *The Hunger Games*. It was the worst World Book Day ever.

The only comfort was that Lisa, April and two of their minions had gone as *Pretty Little Liars*.

So the day could have been even worse.

The day of the exhibition. I'd been worried that they'd cancel it because of the virus and everything, but I texted Rich as soon as I woke up and it was definitely still on. I couldn't wait to see it – the photo of us together. In love. I'd decided this was the night I was going to tell him. Actually say the words, 'I love you.' I wouldn't chicken out this time. The setting was going to be perfect. Far better than a car park anyway.

Neither Mum nor Dad mentioned anything about the show at breakfast so I munched happily on my 5% sugar Cheerios, thinking that they'd forgotten all about it. School was fine but weird, like every day at school is now. Teachers are always telling us things like, 'We'll finish this next week … as long as school's still open,' which is such a crazy thing to hear. They've given us a tonne of homework to do over the weekend too, again, I think with the idea that we'd never finish it, but it could keep us busy next week if we were stuck at home.

At lunch I told Meena that I was going to tell Rich tonight. She freaked out.

'Don't be ridiculous, Meena,' I said. 'We've been over this. There's no reason girls can't say it first.'

'It's not that!' she replied. 'Just don't do it tonight – it's bad luck.'

'What do you mean "it's bad luck?"'

'Friday the 13th?' she said slowly, like I was a complete moron.

I rolled my eyes. 'Superstition is for idiots who don't understand science,' I said primly, momentarily morphing into Anna.

'Don't knock it,' said Meena fake-wisely. 'Bad things happen on Friday 13th.'

I went straight home after school to get changed. I wanted to look nice next to my photo. Rich's mum will probably have Photoshopped it and made my skin all flawless and radiant. I didn't want to stand there looking like some before and after advert.

I'd arranged to meet the gang at Rainston Town Hall at six when the exhibition started, so I had a shower, made myself a Marmite bagel and began writing a note for Mum.

'Sadly, I think you might have forgotten, but…' I wrote, smiling away to myself, only to be interrupted by the sound of a key in the front door.

Damn.

In came Mum and Dad together, also smiling.

'Oh India, funny story,' began Mum. 'I was just looking at my diary to see what time my hair cut was, not that I'm sure I should be having a hair cut at the moment, what with everything…' (*Get to the point!!!*) '…when I saw that it was Rich's mum's exhibition tonight. So I called Dad and he managed to finish up early. I can't believe we nearly missed it! You'd never have forgiven us!'

'I'd have got over it,' I replied, a bit too snidely.

'That's sweet of you to say.' *Clearly not snidely enough.* Mum really does have zero radar for sarcasm.

'Right, well I'll just whip us up a couple of topped oatcakes that we can have in the car and then let's go, shall we?'

Dad looked less than thrilled at the idea of a 'topped

oatcake' for dinner, particularly as he knew that topping was bound to involve cottage cheese and beetroot.

'Here we go,' Mum trilled moments later, 'oatcakes with cottage cheese, roasted beetroot and crunchy soy beans.'

Dad held his at arm's length as if it might suddenly leap out of his palm and attack him. I said I'd already eaten.

On the way there I got texts from Anna and Gillian, both bailing. Damn. I really needed Meena to be there. I didn't want to face this alone. *Glance to the front of the car.* Or rather, not alone.

Thankfully Meena was hovering near the entrance to Rainston Town Hall and her eyes lit up to see me and then expanded into huge globes on seeing my parents seconds behind.

'*What*?' mouthed Meena.

'Tell me about it,' I mouthed back.

From where we were we could see that the hall was already pretty packed. A bubble of excitement floated around in my stomach. *This must be what celebrities feel like every day. Maybe I'll be a celebrity when I grow up? Maybe this will be the start of my path towards celebrity-status? Someone important will see my photo and sign me up there and then...* I clutched my invite getting ready to say my name to the person on the door, but ...

there was no person on the door. Oh. Any old random could walk in. Maybe this was what the most prestigious sort of exhibitions were like? Shuffling inside, I doubted it. Fifty percent of the exhibition seemed to be made up of local homeless people enticed by the idea of free refreshments and a plug-in heater.

I couldn't see Rich anywhere. Disappointed, I grabbed Meena's hand. 'Come on,' I whispered. 'I need to find the photo before my parents do. To see how my dad's going to react.' I imagined him looking at a picture of me and Rich staring intensely into each other's eyes like the couple on the invite. He'd go ballistic seeing us like that. Had we been looking into each other's eyes? I couldn't remember. But there must have been a certain steaminess between us for her to have wanted to use it in her show. Mum and Dad were turning left towards a drinks tray so me and Meena took a right.

Mission: find my picture.

We stopped in front of the first picture we found. It was a really lovely black and white photo of an old couple staring at each other, holding hands. Their wrinkles were deeply etched and their eyes were sunken but they looked so in love. The caption on the plaque next to it read: 'EVERLASTING'.

We moved onto the next photo – black and white again – this was definitely a very classy show. The couple were a bit younger but still old. They were playing cards. The woman was staring at the cards in her hand while the old man peered over the top of his at her. Again, very much in love. The caption this time read: 'SOUL MATES'.

Oooh. I wonder what my caption's going to say!

'We're going the wrong way round,' Meena hissed. 'The people are getting younger. You'll be right at the start so we need to zoom left.'

We missed out photos, six at a time. Sort of like fast-forwarding through a movie.

Skip skip skip.

Couple in their forties staring angrily at each other, eyes flashing: 'BETRAYAL'.

Skip skip skip.

Couple in their early thirties, eyes flashing in a totally different way: 'DESIRE'.

Skip skip skip.

Couple in their twenties from the invite: 'INTENSITY'.

Then, finally we reached it: the photo of me and Rich. I stopped. Frozen to the spot.

The photo was the same size as the others but because it was of me it seemed much, much bigger. Huge, in fact. I was sat on the sofa next to Rich, looking so uncomfortable, a series of angles rather than curves, as if I'd been folded out of origami. My face hadn't been airbrushed flawless. The light was cold and cruel. It was like looking in Meena's make-up mirror. Rich looked just as bad. We weren't looking at each other. We were looking straight ahead. It was all just unbearably awkward. But it wasn't even the photo itself that was making me feel physically sick. It was the caption on the plaque. In black, highly legible letters, was the caption: 'INEXPERIENCE'.

Inexperience!!!!!

Why couldn't we have been 'Everlasting' or 'Timeless' or one of the other good ones? This was so humiliating!!! I wanted the floor to open up and swallow me. Even spontaneous combustion would have been better than this.

I looked at Meena.

She tried to look concerned, but it lasted all of five seconds before, 'Hahahahhahahaha!' just burst out of her mouth. 'I'm sorry,' she said. But then it happened again. 'Hahahahahahahaha!'

I span round, ready to run out into the night, but instead bumped straight into Mum and Dad.

'Oh *here's* the photo,' Mum cried, totally not reading my mood. 'Dad and I have been looking everywhere for it... Oh, it's very good, Andy, don't you think? So *in focus.* Lots of so-called "arty" photos aren't properly in focus. Well, only a tiny bit of the image is and the rest is … well … all blurred. But this is great. I can see every bit of the room. I do wish you were smiling a bit more, though, India. Don't I always say it's important to smile in photos?'

I started zoning out of her babble. It was getting too much. The whole night was getting too much.

Instead I looked at Dad. Gauged how he was reacting. He wasn't looking at the photo. He was looking at the plaque with the title on. Inexperience. A slow smile was spreading over his face.

'India,' there was a tap at my shoulder and Rich was there. His face completely drained of colour. 'I'm so sorry. I had no idea. Mum refused to show me the photos in advance. I texted you…' I pulled my phone out of my pocket. Sure enough, a text from Rich: 'Don't come!!!! X'.

He reached out a hand and I grabbed it like it was a life vest.

'Ah, the couple of the moment,' Dad cried and slapped Rich on the back. Turning to Mum he continued, 'Don't I always say how pleased I am that India's dating Rich?!'

'I want to go home. Now,' I said quietly. 'Please.'

'OK, OK,' Mum said.

'And can we give Meena a lift?'

'Sure.'

We were just out of the door when we were stopped by another cry of, 'India!!'

I turned to see Rich's Mum, flailing her arms around.

'Thank you *so* much for coming ... and you must be India's parents. Hi, I'm Lou. Lovely to meet you.'

I glared laser beams at her.

'Great exhibition,' Mum cooed. 'Really in focus.'

Rich's Mum looked a bit surprised, but then turned her attention to me.

'India, I'm so sorry – I can totally understand why you look angry.' I started to thaw a little. At least she was apologising. 'I have no idea who vandalised your picture ... it is such a travesty. The wanton destruction of art!' OK, now she'd totally lost me.

'We're going home now,' I said flatly. I just wanted to get away from her. Leave her and her stupid photos far behind me.

'Oh, right, bye ... and thanks again. I think we really captured something there.'

Dad was chortling away to himself behind me as we walked to the car. 'Rich Evans, ha ha, Rich Evans,' I heard him muse.

I picked up pace so me and Meena could talk without being overheard.

'What do you think his mum was going on about?' I asked Meena. 'The photo didn't look vandalised.'

Meena gave me a sly smile and pulled something out of her pocket. There, flat on her palm lay a white rectangle with the word 'INEXPERIENCE' on. The plaque! Meena had stolen the plaque! Meena was the vandal. And the world's best friend ever. I could have kissed her.

Instead I gave her a massive hug, virus be damned.

Lying in bed at home I realised I hadn't told Rich I loved him. It hadn't really felt like the right moment.

Meena had been right – Friday 13th *was* unlucky. I think I'm going to have to look a bit more into superstitions. Looks like these people know what's going on.

Monday morning – back at school.

I kept my head down all morning, just in case someone in my year had somehow also been at the exhibition. Seen the photo. Seen the plaque (before Meena stole it). At the start of Geography, April stopped in front of my desk and leant in to whisper, 'Loser.' My heart rate went crazy as I was waiting for her to follow up with something to do with 'inexperience', but nothing came so I beamed back at her and now she thinks I'm even more of a moron than she previously did.

Thank you for calling me loser, April, thank you so much.

Everyone was on edge by lunchtime. Someone from the council had 'popped' in to our English class to ask 'a few little questions' about our home access to laptops. It was the fake casualness of it all that made it so weird. They were trying to pretend it was a totally normal event, which it obviously wasn't. And it was all 'just in case you ever need to work from home', so basically they know they're going to shut the schools, they're just not telling us when.

Working from home would be awful. There's only one computer I'm allowed to use – the desktop on the hall landing. *A shared space is a safe space.* I'd have to work there all day under Mum and Dad's noses. No privacy. No headspace.

And that's not even the worst. Gillian's family don't have a laptop or computer or anything she can use. How on earth is she supposed to get anything done?

Please God don't let it happen.

Please don't let them send us home.

They're sending us home.

Friday is the last day.

Rich was waiting for me outside the gate. He didn't even hover a few metres away. He didn't care who saw him and neither did I. He just walked up to me and snogged me and I snogged him back and I didn't think about virus infected saliva once. He walked me home. We didn't really talk. He just held my hand all the way and told me he'd miss me.

Friday.

The whole last day was spent being trained on different aspects of this home learning app that teachers can set tasks on and that you upload your work to. No one was really concentrating that hard. I spent most of the time staring soulfully at Meena, Anna and Gillian. My friends, my wonderful, wonderful friends, who I was going to be separated from. To make myself feel a bit better, I'd occasionally glance at Lisa and April too, to remind myself that I was at least going to be separated from them as well.

It's only two days into lockdown and everyone's really stressed but pretending not to be.

I've got about five tasks to do a day for school and I've worked out I've got to actually do them well. They've cancelled GCSE exams for Year 11s this year so I guess people will get a mark based on how well they've done over the two years. If they don't bring exams back by next summer, they'll do the same for me and I need to prove I'm better than my rubbish January test scores. I also have to do well in all the tasks as, not having a smart phone, I need to borrow Mum's to photo my work afterwards to upload. I know she then spends a couple of hours reading through everything I've done.

Your magnetic field lines could have been a bit neater in this drawing.

I know it's Maths but the teacher still needs to be able to read your handwriting.

It's hard to take some of the tasks seriously though, particularly if there's an accompanying pre-recorded explanatory video made by the relevant teacher. Some teachers come across exactly as you'd expect. It's almost reassuring. Mrs Johnson's there, barking instructions with about ten cats visible in the background. Mr Major, likewise, no surprises – he's all smiley in a brown cardie, sipping tea from a hand sculpted mug. Others try a bit too hard though. Too many hand gestures. An unexpected purple sofa. Smiles that look like they're about to crack open their faces.

The worst thing is that there are so many things that would be brilliant if the gang were around to share them with, but are only sort of OK by myself. Take this morning – Mr Morretts did a tiny, almost imperceptible burp in the middle of his explanation of a PowerPoint about the eruption of Mount St Helens. He paused for a fraction of a second, looked around himself as if checking to see if anyone had heard and then just carried on, probably because he couldn't be bothered to start again and didn't know how to edit the recording. If I'd been with Meena we'd have wet ourselves. Alone at the landing desk all I managed was a weak 'Ha!'.

Mum's started doing lots of Zoom meetings with work which is really annoying as it means she comes and takes over the landing desktop to do them as the screen's bigger than her laptop and it's the only place in the house with reliable reception. Even when I move into my room to try and get some of the tasks done, I have to listen to her plus her annoying boss plus her annoying colleagues. Mum's really fake at work. Her main contributions to the meeting seem to be saying, 'Great idea!' overly brightly again and again. Dad was dead against Mum working on the landing. He's read somewhere that, in his words, 'weirdos and perverts' can crash Zoom meetings and he doesn't want me to be walking across the landing and catch sight of one on the screen. Honestly.

'I think that's very unlikely, don't you, Andrew?' Mum said patiently.

'They thought a global pandemic was very unlikely and yet here we are,' replied Dad darkly.

'Well, the landing is the only place in the house with decent reception so that's that then.'

When Mum's not 'working' she's baking to try and relax, but it's not giving her the joy it used to. Her 'my madeleines bring all the boys to the yard' was very half-hearted this afternoon. The one thing that seems to be perking her up, however, is that she's convinced that a young guy on our street fancies her.

'He's just very attentive, India. He's always asking how I am. Obviously, I'm not going to do anything about it.' *Obviously, because you're married to my father.* 'But it's flattering. Very flattering.'

Dad seems to be on the verge of a breakdown. Not because of the young guy. Much to Mum's annoyance he doesn't seem jealous about that at all. No, Dad's worked out his dental practice might go bust by the summer and in between looking at various bailout loan options, he's shutting himself in his study and dismantling and rebuilding every bit of his Lego collection.

He's probably also annoyed because we're just on top of each other the whole time. It's unbearable. Every mealtime is now a 'family' mealtime. As if that weren't enough, Mum's even introduced the after-lunch compulsory family walk. 'It'll give us time to take stock. To be in the moment.'

I had a really itchy arm after our walk today. I wonder if I'm becoming physically allergic to my family.

I've worked out that when I'm sat at my desk and look out the window I can see straight into Pete-the-child's bedroom. Not a good realisation. Even worse is the fact that he seems to have realised it too and every now and then he'll write something in massive letters on a huge piece of paper and hold it up to the window for me to read. I know it's for me as it always starts, 'Hey India,' followed by something inane. So far I've had, 'Hey India, check out my rainbows,' with an arrow pointing towards the NHS rainbows he's sellotaped to the bottom of his window. There've also been the classics: 'Hey India, what's your favourite type of pizza?' and 'Hey India, really miss you.'

I haven't replied to any but they just keep on coming.

It's so unfair. I don't want to live across the road from Pete-the-child. I want to live across the road from Meena or Anna or Gillian. Or Rich. I'd love to live across the road from Rich.

Dad would like to swap neighbours too. Lockdown's made him even more convinced that Pete-the-child's parents are Russian spies. It was Clap for Carers last night and Sheila and Jim didn't just open their window and clap like we did. They actually came out and stood in the middle of the road and raised their hands super-high and did absurdly loud clapping.

'Bit over the top,' Mum said afterwards.

'Exactly,' Dad murmured, writing in his notebook. 'That's how you catch them. They try too hard and then they slip up.'

I went on a bike ride. I had to get out of the house. By myself.

Dad's been in such a bad mood that Mum, who's worried about him, suggested that he 'drew his feelings' but Dad snorted at that.

Mum then threatened to get her therapist friend to give him some online sessions, so to avoid that he's agreed to 'sculpt his feelings' instead. He ordered a hundred-pack of modelling balloons and spent yesterday afternoon walking round the house with a wolverine claw that he's made out of five blue balloons and two grey ones by following a YouTube tutorial. I guess that makes his feelings Angry Aging Superhero Mutant.

Mum's also in a foul mood. She wouldn't say why to start with, she was just stomping round the kitchen, flinging things around.

'You want to talk about it, Sammy?' Dad said, putting his arms around her.

'It's just … it's just,' Mum said between sobs.

'What, love? Let it out. Let it out. It's a strange, unsettling time. It's normal to feel worried.'

'It's… it's … the guy down the road. The one I thought liked me. He … he offered to go to the shops for me. In … in case I was vulnerable and self-isolating.' *Sob-choke-sob*. 'Oh, Andy, I think he thought I was … over 65!!!!!!'

'No, no,' Dad stroked Mum's hair, desperately

suppressing the bellowing laugh I could see rising up his body.

'It's true!' *Sob-choke*. 'I must be dressing too old? Do I dress old?'

'No!' me and Dad said at the same time.

'All the same, I think I'm going to dress a bit younger. India, do you have anything that would fit me?'

Dear God.

Although I do have a pair of leggings I could part with…

The start of the Easter holidays and nothing's really different. It's not like I can see anyone now.

I really miss Rich.

I really miss my friends.

To a lesser extent, I also miss fruit.

Mum's decided it's safest if they only go to the shops once a week so all the food she buys now has to last seven days. As a result she's turned into a weird totally opposite version of her former self. We eat pasta at least once a day and if my hand stretches towards the fruit bowl she's all, 'You've already had an apple today, hands off, have a biscuit instead.'

Tuesday morning.

I got a text from Rich. The words 'meeting ID' followed by a string of numbers. Then 'password' and some more numbers and then a 'x'.

'? X' I texted back.

'I've set up a Zoom meeting. I have to see you. I miss you so much. It's for 1.30pm today. Can you get on a computer then? x'

1.30pm… That's family walk time…

'Yes,' I replied. I had to see him. I'd make it work.

We had lunch at 12.45. I ate my fish finger wrap in record time and then made a big show of *Is that the time? What a lovely day. Shame to waste it. Off you go then…*

'Aren't you coming too?' asked Dad.

'Not today,' I replied, attempting to look rueful. 'I've … (*think of plausible excuse … come on, brain*) … got online Art Club.'

'Online Art Club?' repeated Mum suspiciously.

'Yup, online Art club.' *No point backing down now.* 'School set it up. To … you know … help our emotional wellbeing. We're … drawing our feelings about Covid.'

Too much information.

'Oh… That sounds like a very good idea. I look forward to seeing what you produce!'

Damn.

It was 1:20 when I herded them out the door. Time for a quick ten-minute sketch of a girl looking sad holding something resembling a football with spikes and then I was Zoom ready. I sat down at the 'family' computer in the window alcove of the landing and turned it on. I'd watched Mum do it for work, so I knew how to launch the app etc.

My face appeared on the screen – blanched out with my nose looking double normal width (I hope). Aggghhhh. Hideous. I wanted to run to the bathroom to put on some more make-up but there was no time.

Before I knew it Rich had 'admitted me to the meeting' and there he was. The face I'd been missing so much these past weeks. The eyes. The smile.

I clicked on gallery mode so I could see us side by side. Imagine we were in the same room. Sitting next to each other. He was in his bedroom. His mum clearly didn't have the same ridiculous rules.

'Hey,' he said.

'He—' I started to reply,' but then stopped. What was happening? Rich was backing away from the screen. Did I look so hideous that he'd decided to leg it? *She's not what I remembered, I'm off…*

He backed away still further and then stopped. And that's when I realised … he had no top on. Jeans, yes, but no top. Why the hell was Rich Evans staring out at me topless from the big monitor on the hall landing!?!! I'd never even seen his body before. Not undressed. It wasn't bad or anything but it wasn't amazing. Not like the bodies of guys who take their tops off whatever the weather just to show off the six-pack they've wasted their whole life at the gym making. And he was looking horrifically awkward. Like someone was standing out of shot saying 'show her your torso or the kitten gets it'.

'What's going on?' I asked, seriously weirded out.

'Nothing much,' he said, trying to tense his biceps.

'Why don't you have a top on?' I asked.

'Just kind of felt like it,' he stuttered.

God, did he expect me to reciprocate? There was no way I was stripping my top off in front of the hall landing window. I didn't really want Rich seeing me in my bra, let alone Pete-the-child across the road.

'Rich…'

'Oh, I'm sorry, India, I'm an idiot,' he said, face crumpling, biceps slumping. 'Alex said it would be a good idea.'

Alex is one of his best mates. Not terribly smart.

'He said it'd make me look sexy … you know. He said you might be put off me by the whole "inexperience"

235

thing so I should … well … try to look sexy so you didn't go off me.'

Rich stood there, topless, furiously blushing, real and vulnerable and the words just burst out of my mouth.

'I couldn't go off you. I love you.'

Not quite how I'd planned to tell him.

'Really?' he said, and the corners of his mouth flicked up and I thought he was going to smile. But he didn't. Other facial muscles kicked in and suddenly he looked terrified. Oh no! I'd done it. Meena was right. I'd scared him off. His eyes were widening. But they didn't seem to be looking at me. They were focusing just past my left ear.

What the hell? I tell him I love him and he's looking past my left ear? I changed my attention from the rectangle with Rich in it to the rectangle of me on the screen. To what Rich was looking at.

Noooooo. It couldn't be. In the back of the shot, behind me, Dad was climbing the stairs. He was on the top step. He'd reached the landing…

'Indiaaaaaaa!!!!!' Dad's squeal ripped open the air. He was staring at the screen – finger jabbing.

No. no. NO!!! How the hell had that happened? How come I hadn't heard them come back? Why were they back so soon?

'Samantha!!!!!!!! Oh my God! India, shut it down

shut it down. Your Art Club has a pervert Zoom crasher. Actually, wait a minute. Don't shut it. Keep it open... Do they have a user ID? Let's report this pervert to the police. Seems to start with an R... *Close your screen, Rich*. I wanted to scream. *End the meeting!* But Rich was frozen to the spot, paralysed with fear. As was I.

'R-i-ch,' Dad was edging closer, reading the letters under Rich's image. 'Rich Evans!!!! RICH EVANS!!!' he exploded, shaking his fist at the screen, looking like he might try and dive into the computer itself and throttle the pixilated version of my boyfriend. 'How DARE you try and have a ... a ... *lewd* call with my daughter!!!!! You're a cunning devil, I'll give you that. You try and throw me off the scent with all that "inexperience" rubbish... Ha!... Think you can take Andrew Smythe for a fool, do you! You're a wolf in sheep's clothing, that's what you are. A wolf in sheep's clothing! I forbid you to see India any more and ... I'm ... I'm leaving the band!!!!!!!'

'No!!!!!!!!!' Rich's cry was cut off as Dad wrenched the plug from the wall.

'And, India, you're grounded!'

As if that made any difference to my current existence.

I spent the rest of the afternoon and evening in my room. I wasn't hungry. I kept checking my phone for a text from Rich, saying … I don't know … something. Actually I do know, I know exactly what I wanted it to say. I wanted it to say that he loved me too. That the 'Noooooo!' was because he'd been banned from seeing me rather than because Dad had left his band.

But my phone sat there. Silent.

No beeps.

No phone call.

Nothing.

Wednesday. Still nothing from Rich.

Dad was acting like a complete psycho. Every time I left my room, he was suddenly there, next to me, shooting glances in all directions to see if I'd secretly hidden a topless Rich in the utility room or behind the sofa.

It was all getting too much.

I called Meena, looking for help/comfort.

Her initial reaction was neither helpful nor comforting.

'He had his top off? Hahahahahahaha… To try to impress you? Hahahahahahaha… And your Dad saw? Hahahahahahahaha.'

When she'd finished laughing her head off, I steered her back to the important stuff.

'But what does it mean?' I asked. 'I said "I love you" and he didn't say anything back.'

'It's not good,' Meena agreed. 'But, to be fair, he didn't have a chance to say it back as your Dad came up the stairs. Hahahahahahaha.'

'But,' I said, ignoring her cackling laughter, 'he hasn't texted me or called me or anything since.'

'Maybe he's lost his phone?'

'Nobody's going out. He can't have lost his phone in his room. Or if he did, he's had over twenty-four hours to find it again.'

'Maybe he's been kidnapped?'

'Meena!'

'What do you want me to say? I was trying to spare your feelings. It doesn't look good, OK? It doesn't look good at all.'

With that we said goodbye and I hung up with a lump in my throat.

Thursday.

Hours dragged. I read a whole book, checked my

phone about a zillion times and made three dog balloon animals and it wasn't even lunchtime. The afternoon went by even slower. It was like I was experiencing a time warp, a week masquerading as a few hours.

Eventually it was 8pm – time to clap. I went to my room and opened the window. Pete-the-child was already leaning out of his window on the other side of the street and he waved enthusiastically as soon as he saw me. His parents were out in the middle of the road, pacing up and down, flexing their hands, limbering up. They weren't the only ones outside today. I recognised some other families from further down the street. The Taylors from number 72 and the Bhatias from number 67. Their kids too. A bit like an impromptu street party. In the middle of them was the keenest guy ever. He was carrying a huge homemade rainbow banner about a metre across. He put the (possibly) Russians to shame. I couldn't see the face of this keen bean as it was hidden behind the banner, but I'd have bet it was Mike from number 33. He's always the one with a cardboard cut-out of the Queen for royal weddings and a blow-up Santa for Christmas.

A smatter of applause began at the top of the street and then we all joined in. It built in volume until all our hands were stinging. Then, as it reached its peak, banner guy started to walk towards my house. It was a weird walk. Almost a scuttle. It reminded me of a crab on the beach. Like he was trying to be stealthy but there's only so much stealth that can be achieved with an oversized rainbow instead of a head. There's a reason ninjas don't typically carry banners. Anyway he kept scuttling forward until he was directly under my window.

Go away, Mike from number 33. I've always found you a bit creepy. There was something about the way he said, 'Would you like a mer-ingue?' at the last actual street party that made my skin crawl.

But he didn't go. Instead he lowered his rainbow to reveal blue eyes, dimples and a majestic forehead. Not creepy Mike at all. It was Rich. Rich Evans was standing beneath my window smiling up at me. He'd gone undercover. Risking death-by-Dad just to see me. He was basically Romeo. All we needed was a balcony. I beamed back at him.

Then, eyes flitting from side to side as if on the lookout for predators, he turned the banner round. On the other side, in place of the rainbow was some writing.

Huge black letters spelling out:

'I love you, India Smythe.'

It took a few seconds for my brain to compute. To take it all in.

He loves me!

Rich Evans loves me!

I love you too! I mouthed back. Rich wrinkled up his forehead. I don't think he could lip-read either.

Throwing caution to the wind, I opened my window even further, straining the hinges and yelled at the top of my lungs, 'I love you too!'

Unfortunately it was at the exact moment when the clapping stopped so I was yelling into a silent street. Everyone was twisting their heads to see what was going on. Normally I would have been dying from embarrassment, but this time I wasn't. I was so euphoric that I started cracking up instead.

Then two things happened at the exact same time.

First, a movement from across the street caught my eye.

Pete-the-child was holding a new piece of paper up to his window.

More big black lettering. This time it read:

'I knew it!'

Second, Dad, having heard my yelled declaration of love and, recognising my voice, was out the front door. He spotted Rich instantly and was after him with a growl. Rich took one look at my crazy father and was off, pegging it down the road. My last glimpse of them was of my boyfriend (who I love and who loves me) silhouetted against the horizon closely followed by my raging father. The two men in my life. Disappearing into the sunset together.

I started laughing again. This is a crazy time. A truly, truly crazy time. But somehow I know I'll get through it. We all will.

And I feel happy.

Truly happy.

Because India Smythe is in love.

ACKNOWLEDGMENTS

Huge thanks to my husband for his boundless enthusiasm and encouragement. Thanks to my agent, Jane Turnbull, for really believing in India Smythe. Thanks to Earl, my incredible editor. Thanks to Nina Duckworth for her fantastic artwork and to Anne Glenn for the overall cover design. Thanks to all my teen readers and reviewers and to the amazing librarians who helped connect us, including Lucas Maxwell, Lucy Atherton, Helen Cleaves, Alison Martino and Edward Benton. Thanks to Kirsty Ridge for her eagle-eyed proof reading. And, finally, thanks to my family.

Sarah Govett graduated with a First in Law from Trinity College, Oxford. After qualifying as a solicitor she set up her own tutoring agency before turning her energies to writing. Her first trilogy, *The Territory*, won the Trinity Schools Book Award and the Gateshead Teen Book Award and was described by the *Guardian* Children's Books site as 'the 1984 of our time'. It has now been optioned for TV.

Sarah is an in-demand speaker at secondary schools and has appeared at the Southbank Literature Festival, the Edinburgh International Book Festival, the Bradford Literature Festival and the Godolphin Literature Festival.

She lives in London with her husband and three young children.

Have you read the first India Smythe book?

INDIA SMYTHE STANDS UP

Fourteen-year-old India Smythe has caught the eye of Ennis, the hottest boy at St Joseph's. But nothing's ever easy when you're dealing with horrific teachers, a dad who's convinced every boy is a sex pest, a best friend who talks you into embarrassing makeovers to look good on Insta and the odd kissing-induced hospitalisation.

And does India even want Ennis?

Or should she risk social relegation and go for the orchestra geek with the extra-long forehead who she actually enjoys talking to?

'The new YA comedy teens need… when a book like *India Smythe Stands Up* comes along you need to get it into as many hands as possible'
Lucas Maxwell, BookRiot

'One of the funniest protagonists since … well … ever! She fits in with Bridget Jones and Georgia Nicolson. The perfect antidote to the grim, grey times in which we find ourselves' *Teen Librarian*

'A genuinely laugh-out-loud funny book with a fresh authentic voice' *Teach Secondary Magazine*

'Laugh-out-loud story with a thoughtful subtext' *Books for Keeps*

THE TERRITORY
(a dystopian trilogy)

Noa Blake is just another normal 15 year old with exams looming. Except in The Territory normal isn't normal. The richest children have a node on the back of their necks and can download information, bypassing the need to study.

In a flooded world of dwindling resources, Noa and the other 'Norms' have their work cut out even to compete. And competing is everything – because everyone who fails the exams will be shipped off to the Wetlands, which means a life of misery, if not certain death.

But how to focus when your heart is being torn in two directions at once?

WINNER OF THE TSBA 2018

'The 1984 of our time' the *Guardian* children's books

'A truly exceptional novel' *Booktrust*

'Thrilling and thought-provoking' *The Times*

'Gripping dystopia with a keen political edge'
Imogen Russell Williams, *Metro*

Coming 2021:
WE GO ON FOREVER
(a new dystopian series)

Want to be the first to hear about
Sarah's upcoming books?

Join the mailing list through her website:
www.sarahgovett.com
Or follow her on Instagram/twitter @sarahgovett